CHRONICLES of the UNICORN KINGDOM

Destiny

Kyle Rawleigh

Illustrated by Linda Brisson

CLAY BRIDGES
P R E S S

Chronicles of the Unicorn Kingdom
Destiny

Published by Clay Bridges Press in Houston, TX
www.ClayBridgesPress.com

ISBN: 978-1-68488-078-2 pb
ISBN: 978-1-68488-079-9 hb
eISBN: 978-1-68488-080-5

Special Sales: Most Clay Bridges titles are available in special quantity discounts. Custom imprinting or excerpting can also be done to fit special needs. Contact Clay Bridges at Info@ClayBridgesPress.com

For Mrs. Paulson's class of 2022, and the rest of our dedicated readers.

For Mrs. Paulson's class of 2022, and the rest of our dedicated readers.

CONTENTS

CHAPTER 1

THE FIB

Liv stood in her basement. Many eyes were trained on her, waiting for her to tell them what to do. Her sisters, Ava and Claire, were there, along with her dog Leo, her two-year-old brother Mason, and their friend Grace. Even young Mason could tell they were all in a really tough situation.

I can't believe Reagan is a vampire, Liv thought to herself. *And I can't believe we left her there.* Liv thought about what King Andrew told her right before they used the orb to teleport back to her basement. "Nobody can take your hope away from you—you have to choose to give it up."

Liv had never given up on anything in her entire life—and she wasn't about to start today.

"Here is what we're going to do," Liv started. "We are going to trick our parents. We are going to convince them that we are going to spend the rest of today and tonight at someone's house. But we need to make sure they all think we're in different places, so nobody asks any questions."

"You mean we are going to lie to our parents?" Claire asked. "You know what Dad says about where liars go."

"It's more of a fib," Liv answered. "We'll tell our parents and Reagan's parents that we are all going to spend today and tonight at Grace's house. Grace will tell her parents we are all staying at Reagan's. That way, no parents will expect us to be at their house, and hopefully, nobody will notice we're gone."

"How is Reagan supposed to call her parents and tell them she's sleeping at my house *when she's a vampire*?" Grace shouted.

"And what about Mason?" Ava asked. "He's only two. Mom would never agree to let him sleep over somewhere. He's too little."

"All good points," Liv replied. "Let's take this one step at a time. I will call Reagan's house and pretend I'm her. I'll let her parents know we're staying at Grace's. Grace, you need to call your parents and tell them we're staying at Reagan's."

Grace crossed her arms. "I don't know about this, Liv."

"It's 5:00 a.m. here right now. If we can convince our parents, we could be in the Unicorn Kingdom by 7:30 a.m. That would give us about 24 hours before anyone starts to wonder where we are."

Ava raised her eyebrows in surprise. "Twenty-four hours? That's almost a month in Unicorn Kingdom time."

"We are going to need every second of it to fix this," Liv answered. "We've got some time to kill before Mom and Dad wake up. Let's grab some breakfast and get packed to prepare for this."

Everyone went upstairs. It was still pitch black outside. During the winter in Minnesota, the sun rises late. Liv made some breakfast to try to fill everyone's tummy for what would be the longest trip they had ever taken to the Unicorn Kingdom. She made her mom and dad's favorite breakfast to try to butter them up and convince them to let Mason sleep over at Grace's, even though they'd actually be trying to save Reagan and all their friends from a vampire invasion two worlds away.

The girls and Mason filled their stomachs with bacon and eggs and then sprang into action, finding snacks and supplies to bring with them on their adventure. While everyone was getting their supplies organized, Liv walked two huge plates of bacon and eggs up to her mom and dad to treat them to breakfast in bed.

The moment she opened the door her dad snapped up in his bed. "I smell bacon!" he said.

Liv's dad loves bacon.

"What's all this, honey?" her mom asked.

Liv put on her biggest smile. "We made you breakfast!"

"That is so sweet," her mom replied.

"Gimme!" her Dad yelled. "Thanks, Liv!"

Liv was an expert at trying to get what she wanted from her parents. She knew that now was the best shot she had to try to get it.

"Yeah. We were talking last night about how you guys work so hard all the time and never really get a day off," Liv said.

"Well, a morning off of making breakfast is a dream come true," her mom answered. Her dad was too busy stuffing his face with bacon to talk, but he gave her a thumbs up.

"We were actually thinking of giving you guys the whole day off," Liv said, still smiling.

"What do you mean?" Mom asked.

"We were thinking we'd all head to Grace's and bring Mason with us to hang out for the day. Grace's mom even said he could spend the night with us."

"Hah! No way," Mom said. "He's too little."

"Mom, when is the last time you guys had a day to yourselves?"

Liv's dad finally spoke up. "How old are you?" he asked.

"Dad, you know I'm 13."

"Then it's been 13 years since we've had a day off."

Liv rolled her eyes at him like she always did for his dad jokes.

"Did Grace's mom actually say you all could crash there? Even Mason?" Mom asked.

"Yep!" Liv lied.

"And you can bring your phone with you and call us if anything goes wrong or you need us to come and get him, right?" Dad asked.

"Yep!" Liv lied again.

Mom smacked Liv's dad on the shoulder. "He can't stay the night. He's too little."

"Fine," Dad said. "You guys can go hang out, but I'll be there tonight to pick up Mason at 8:00."

"Sounds good. Thanks!" Liv said, knowing this was an argument she wasn't going to win.

That doesn't sound good! How are we going to do this? Liv thought to herself as she walked back downstairs. It was 7:00 a.m. now, time for the next part of the plan.

"Did it work?" Ava asked her big sister.

"We got permission to have Mason there until 8:00 o'clock tonight. I'll bring my phone with me to the Unicorn Kingdom and try calling Dad at 8:00 to tell him Mason fell asleep. Maybe he'll just let Mason stay the night."

"I can't handle all the lies!" Claire wailed.

Once Liv got back to the basement, she started digging through Reagan's things and found her phone. Lucky for Liv, she spent so much time with Reagan that she knew how to unlock her cell phone. She went to Reagan's "favorites," tapped "Mom," and walked upstairs to lie to Reagan's parents about where her daughter was going to be for the next 24 hours.

"Looks like we're doing this," Ava said. "Grace, I think you'd better make the call too."

Grace grabbed her phone and walked upstairs to lie to her mom as well.

"We are going to get in so much trouble," Claire said. "Dad always finds out when we lie."

"Well, is it okay if we're lying to try to help our friend?" Ava asked.

"I'm pretty sure it isn't," Clair responded quickly.

Just then, Liv walked back downstairs. "That was surprisingly way easier than I thought. Reagan's mom said she was all good with it. She didn't even seem to notice it was me and not her own daughter!"

"Don't make a habit of it," Claire said as she frowned at her biggest sister.

Not long after that, Grace walked down the stairs. "It's done. I'm all clear until tomorrow morning."

The girls quickly realized that for a 24–hour day trip, one SUSK (Secret Unicorn Survival Kit) wasn't going to be enough. Ava and Claire emptied their school bags and filled them with snacks, drinks, and a few other supplies, such as flashlights and extra clothes.

"Let's head to the park," Liv said. "Once the coast is clear, we'll use the orb to get back to the Unicorn Kingdom and find out how to save Reagan."

"And everyone else," Ava added nervously. She was holding the Sword of Ridder, the ancient weapon that she and only she could use to destroy Luca and rid the world of vampires.

Everyone got dressed and went outside to start walking to the park on a very chilly Minnesota winter morning. They made it to the nearby park in next to no time. Liv looked

around to make sure there was nobody nearby. Snow-covered playgrounds normally aren't very busy in the winter. The coast was clear.

Liv reached into her SUSK and pulled out the green orb that Ava recovered after they met Luca. "Everybody hang on tight."

Without saying a word, they all grabbed on. Leo nestled up next to Liv's leg like he always did, and she put her hand on his head.

"I wish we were in the Unicorn Kingdom," Liv stated.

CHapTer 2

WHAT DID WE MISS?

Within moments, everyone was back in the courtyard just outside the palace of the Unicorn Kingdom. They were prepared for their toughest adventure yet and eager to find a way to save Reagan.

"Where do we even start?" Leo asked.

Liv was in such a hurry that she had already started walking toward the palace. She looked over her shoulder and said, "We need to talk to King Andrew." As Liv made her way to the palace, she noticed that there were many elves around with the unicorns. It looked like the elves were still staying in the Unicorn Kingdom for safekeeping.

The moment the children and Leo walked into the large throne room inside the palace, Brooke and Sparkles came running up to them. "Thank goodness you're back!" Brooke said.

Liv felt like she had just seen them a few hours ago. But she remembered that the handful of hours that had passed since they arrived home ate breakfast, lied to their parents, and teleported back was several days in the Unicorn Kingdom.

"What did we miss?" Liv asked.

From his throne, King Andrew spoke up immediately. Everyone walked over to him to listen.

"A lot has already happened since you left," he began. "The vampires still have three orbs. We haven't been able to get any of them back, but we've had some of the elves track their movement. We know where they are."

Liv threw the green orb she had used to teleport them to the Unicorn Kingdom toward Ava. Once it was close to her, it floated to the hilt and embedded itself back into the Sword of Ridder. Ava then grabbed the blue orb and made sure it locked itself in place as well.

"So we've got two of the orbs, and you know where the other three are," Liv said. "That sounds like good news to me."

"That's about as good as our news gets right now," chimed in Neon, the powerful, brave unicorn.

"Unfortunately, he isn't wrong," King Andrew said. "The three orbs we need to get back so Ava can slay Luca with the Sword of Ridder are very well protected."

Liv looked over at Ava when King Andrew talked about her slaying the vampire. She saw Ava nervously look down at her feet.

"They moved some orbs around on us," the King continued. "The pink orb that belongs to our kingdom was sent to the Goblin Kingdom to be protected."

"Let me guess," Claire said. "Everyone in the Goblin Kingdom is still turned into vampires?"

"Yes." King Andrew answered. "And don't forget that the trolls have been turned into vampires as well. Getting in and out of there is going to be very dangerous. The purple orb from the elves was actually returned to the Elven Kingdom."

"All the elves are here, aren't they?" Liv asked.

King Andrew nodded. "Yes, the ones that are left are here. Reagan is in the Elven Kingdom with George the Dragon and an army of vampires. Most of the elves came here. The ones who stayed weren't able to defend their kingdom. Reagan, George the Dragon, and the vampires just walked in and took over."

Liv had a very worried look on her face. "Are you sure everyone was turned into vampires?"

Neon shook his head. "We don't know about the Historian, but most likely, everyone else has turned. The Historian said nobody in his position had ever abandoned the library, and he wasn't going to be the first."

"Is he all right?" Liv asked.

"We don't know," Neon answered.

Liv was starting to feel a little discouraged, but then she remembered King Andrew's wise words. *Nobody can take hope away from you. You have to choose to give it up.* She tried to stay positive. "Where is the Dwarven orb?" she asked.

"The golden orb of the Dwarves was locked in a small, circular metal box and placed on a necklace that hangs around Luca's neck. Right now, he is still sitting in the Dwarven Kingdom with the rest of his vampire army," King Andrew replied.

"And what about the mermaids?" Ava questioned King Andrew.

"Since they live underwater off the coast, they are safe as far as we know. But we aren't certain."

Liv looked around and saw the worried looks on everyone's faces. "So the only things we know for sure is that we have two of the five orbs we need and that everyone inside the Unicorn Kingdom is safe. Everyone outside this kingdom we would consider to be a vampire, except maybe the mermaids. We're outnumbered. And if I'm not mistaken, we're also surrounded."

King Andrew nodded. "It's safe to say that as we speak, Luca is planning a final attack to get the last two orbs in his possession. Then he will turn the rest of us into vampires."

"We need a plan, and we need to get going fast," Claire said.

Neon stepped up next to King Andrew. "We have started thinking about how to do this, but I don't think you guys are going to like it."

"We're going to need to split up," King Andrew said bluntly.

"No. No way. Absolutely not," Liv answered. "Last time we did that, Reagan was turned into a vampire. We aren't doing that ever again."

"Just like before, time is not on our side and we don't we don't have a choice," Neon replied. "Every moment we stand here we're a moment closer to a final invasion. It will be the one that turns all of us into vampires and ends this world as we know it."

Ava walked over to Liv and whispered in her ear. "He's right, Liv. This is all scary, but if we're going to fix this and save Reagan, splitting up to get it done faster is going to be our best shot. At least hear them out."

Liv looked at Ava and nodded. Then she turned back to Neon. "So what do we do?"

Neon spoke up. "Sparkles, Grace, you, and Moonbeam are going to sneak into the Goblin Kingdom and recover the orb that's hidden there. We thought with Moonbeam's invisibility and Sparkles' flying power; you'd have the best chance of getting in and out quickly and quietly."

"And the best chance of escaping," King Andrew added. "The rest of us are going to head north to the Elven Kingdom. We're going to be in for a very dangerous fight to get the orb back from Reagan."

"Reagan isn't dangerous!" Liv shouted, defending her friend. "It isn't even her fault this happened to her."

"She's a vampire now," King Andrew replied. Liv, she *is* dangerous. But she isn't the one I'm worried about. George is the one. I thought dragons were the strongest creatures here, but vampires might be just as dangerous. George is now a vampire dragon. We don't even know what he's capable of at this point."

"Whether it is good or bad news, George is still loyal to Reagan," Neon chimed in. "I'm hoping that's a good thing somehow."

"All right, so we split up," Liv agreed. "*If* Grace and I can get the orb back from the Goblin Kingdom, and *if* you guys are able to get the orb back from Reagan and George, then what do we do?"

Neon and King Andrew both looked at each other. They were silent for a few moments. It almost seemed to Liv that neither of them wanted to be the one to tell the girls, Leo and Mason, the last part of the plan.

After an uncomfortable silence, King Andrew finally spoke up. "We fully expect that we're going to lose some members of our army in the fight with Reagan and George. Even if we're able to get the orb back, it will come at a cost. There will be a lot of vampires there, and some of our army will likely be turned into vampires along the way. *When* you get the orb from the Goblin Kingdom and *when* we get Reagan's, everyone that's left is going to head to the Dwarven Kingdom for the last stand."

"Last stand?" Claire asked, sounding concerned.

Neon started talking again. Liv noticed a glimmer of evil in his eyes. His voice sounded a little scary, kind of like it did before he earned their trust. "Everyone who is left will come with us to the Dwarven Kingdom. We'll do anything we can to get the final orb from Luca and give it to Ava."

"Once Ava has the final orb, the Sword of Ridder will work to destroy Luca once and for all," King Andrew said confidently.

"We're going to bring this fight straight to his doorstep," Neon said. "When the dust settles, this will all be over one way or another. I am going to make Luca pay for what he did to Star and everyone else." Neon sounded even angrier than before.

"I hate this plan," Liv said. "I hate every single thing about this plan. It's too dangerous."

King Andrew nodded. "I completely agree. You all have done plenty for us, and nobody is making you stay. You don't owe us anything."

Ava spoke up loudly for the first time since they started talking. "We're not leaving you guys. I'm the only one who can hold this stupid sword. I don't know why it picked me, but I'm going to use it to save you." With a big smile on her face, she looked at her big sister and said, "We got this, Liv."

Liv shook her head again, still not liking it. But she realized that if they were going to save Reagan and their magical world, she didn't have much of a choice.

"So when Moonbeam, Grace, Sparkles, and I get our orb, what do we do next?" Liv asked.

"You come back here," King Andrew responded, "and we'll do the same once we get the orb back from Reagan."

Liv nodded. "Okay. One last question. When do we start?"

"Dawn," Neon replied.

After getting brought up to speed, the girls tried to get settled in for the night. It was obvious that it would be nearly impossible to get any rest. They were happy they at least had a plan, but there were still many unanswered questions that raced through their brains. It was a struggle to calm down their minds.

Liv was lying on the ground surrounded by her little brother, her dog, her two sisters, and Grace. She crossed her arms in frustration and said, "I still hate that we're splitting up."

Grace shifted around uncomfortably on the ground. "I know. But it's our only choice. We don't have time to stick together. It'll be okay, Liv."

Liv shook her head. "I hope so. But my dad always says that hope isn't a plan. I'm just worried it might not work."

"Yeah, but we never know for sure if our plans are going to work," Grace pointed out.

"True."

"This bedtime feels different," Claire said. "I don't like it when bedtime feels different." She knew she wasn't the baby of the family any longer since Mason was only two, but she couldn't help but feel afraid and a bit off about this whole thing. So did Liv.

Ava was holding the Sword of Ridder close to her like she always did since she had pulled it out of the statue. She thought about how in Earth time it was only about 12 hours ago that she had first held the sword. She remembered how she didn't expect to budge it from the statue it was stuck in. Even though it was yesterday, it felt like forever ago. As she sat with her friends and family, she nervously tapped the hilt of the sword on the ground. "You guys are thinking about this all wrong," she said. "There is no sense getting worked up and worrying about stuff that hasn't even happened yet."

Liv glanced up at her sister and nodded. "Also true." Because Liv was the oldest, she always felt responsible for her siblings. Sometimes Ava's willingness to charge into things head first without thinking drove her crazy, but she was glad Ava was so brave.

"Yeah, Liv, it's kind of like a dance," Claire said. "Mom is always telling you to stop worrying about messing up and focus on the little things you can do right."

A smile spread across Ava's face. "Exactly! Instead of worrying about all the stuff that might go wrong, let's think about what we can do to make sure things go right. What if it works? What if we win?"

Claire corrected Ava. "Not *if* we win—*when* we win."

Ava responded, getting very excited, "When we win, everyone—Reagan, George the Dragon, Star, and all the others who have been bitten—will go back to normal. And we'll save this place."

"When we win, maybe they'll build a statue of Ava holding the sword like they did for Ridder," Liv said.

"Maybe they'll build a statue of all of us," Ava laughed. "Maybe the Historian will write a story about us that'll live on forever in that library Liv went to."

And just like that, Liv's mind went back into worry mode. Thinking of the Historian reminded her of what he said as she left. *Whether you succeed or fail, you and your friends will wind up being a very important part of the history I document. If you fail, I fear there will be nobody left to read about what happens.*

"Can you guys promise me something?" Liv asked.

"Duh!" Ava said, still trying to make light of the situation.

"Promise me you guys will get the orb back from Reagan and meet me back here."

"We will if you will," Claire told Liv.

"And another thing," Liv said. "When you get there, I need you to check on the Historian, okay? We wouldn't have stood a chance if it wasn't for him. I'd like to know if he's okay or not."

"Didn't you say the library was giant and dark and that he's the only one in there?" Claire asked.

"Yep."

"Sounds creepy," Ava answered. "So you want us to walk into a dark, spooky library with an elf we've never met who could be a vampire now? Sounds kind of risky coming from the person who doesn't even want us to split up."

"It might be," Liv said, "but I got to know him, and if the roles were reversed, I don't think he would leave any of us behind. He'd try to help us. Just check it out for me, okay?"

"Fine, we'll do it," Ava promised.

Mason let out a snore.

"Looks like we bored the little guy to sleep," Grace said.

Liv looked at her little brother sleeping on the ground, snuggled up with Leo. She admired how Mason was kind of oblivious to what was going on. He was a smart kid and could sense they were going to do something dangerous. But if he knew how dangerous this is, he probably wouldn't be out cold right now.

"We can't bring him with us for this part," Liv said as she stroked his hair. "Leo, I think you should stay here with him."

Even though Leo had the ability to talk, he just hung his head and made a whining sound.

"Sorry, bud. It's just going to be too dangerous for Mason. If he stays here with you, I know you'll do a good job of taking care of him until we get back," Liv said reassuringly.

"All right. We'll stay here," Leo said. We totally won't follow you or get into any trouble."

Liv shot a stern look at her dog. "Leo, promise me you'll stay here and take care of Mason like a good dog."

"Okay. I pwomise," he said.

Ava giggled. "Leo, did you say pwomise?"

"Promise, Leo, with an *R*," Liv said.

Liv wasn't sure if dogs could actually let out a sigh or not, but she was pretty sure her dog let out a big, obnoxious sigh and then said, "Fine. I promise. With an *R*."

Knowing her brother and dog were going to be safe and sound felt like Liv's first win since they had arrived earlier that day.

Things quieted down a bit after that, and everyone seemed to relax. Liv had fallen asleep, but Neon's familiar voice startled her awake. As she blinked the sleep out of her eyes, she noticed the sun starting to rise. She couldn't believe how normal the morning felt even though many bad things were about to happen in this world. Their plan was going to be very dangerous.

As the sun was coming up, the pinkish Unicorn Kingdom sky was beautiful. If they didn't have to save the world, it would've been a perfect day to spend with their unicorns.

"We've got a world to save. Let's get to work," Neon said.

CHaPTer 3

TAKING THE HIGH ROAD

The girls didn't have much time for goodbyes. It was time to move. They gave each other a quick hug.

"Be careful," Liv told her sisters.

"We will. You do the same," Claire answered as she stopped hugging her biggest sister.

Liv turned to Leo. "Remember, you promised to stay here and keep Mason safe."

Leo rolled his doggy eyes at Liv.

"Promised with an *R*," Ava reminded her dog.

"Okay, okay. I get it," Leo replied, sounding annoyed.

With that, Liv hopped on Moonbeam's back. They started to trot away with Grace and Sparkles right behind them. Liv turned around and yelled over her shoulder, "I love you!"

"Love you too!" Ava and Claire hollered back.

Liv still hated this plan, but all she could control now was her part of it. She needed to get to the Goblin Kingdom and get the orb back to the Unicorn Kingdom safely. If anything went wrong between now and then, she'd have to figure that out later. Breaking it down into smaller parts always helped Liv feel less anxious in situations like this.

Step 1 – Get to the Goblin Kingdom, she told herself.

As she rode with Grace, Sparkles, and Moonbeam, she already realized her first problem. The fastest, safest way to get to the Goblin Kingdom was to take a passage that tunneled underneath some very tall mountains. They stood between the Unicorn Kingdom and the land that used to be run by General Gorum before he was turned into a vampire.

That passage was sealed off last year when Gork and the trolls sacrificed themselves, willingly being turned into vampires so Liv and Claire could escape an angry horde of vampire goblins. King Andrew used his stun power to blast the roof of the cave, causing rocks to collapse and blocking the passageway.

"We're going to need to go over the mountains to get there and back," Liv said.

"That'll be easy enough for us," Sparkles said as she flapped her wings, indicating she could easily fly over them.

The mountains were enormous. Liv could already see them in the distance even though they were still very far away. She could see that the tops were still covered in snow, just like the last couple of times she had been there.

"Yeah, easy for you," Liv said. "That's sure to be dangerous for Moonbeam and me."

Within a few hours, they arrived at the base of the mountains. Liv always knew they were steep and looked dangerous, but she had never needed to climb them. Now that she had to find a way over and was looking more closely, it looked like it was going to be almost impossible.

"Where do we even start?" Liv asked.

"It's hard to tell from down here," Moonbeam responded. "Sparkles, do you think you could fly up and see if you can find a way for us to get over?"

Sparkles' wings were already flapping. She was heading up as she said, "You got it. We'll be back soon."

Liv watched as Sparkles and Grace went up so high that they looked like small birds. A while later, they landed back on the ground. As soon as they got back, Grace was shivering.

"It's freezing up there," she said.

Sparkles nodded and said, "But we did find a path. Well, sort of a path anyway."

"What is 'sort of a path'?" Liv asked.

"Well, there is definitely a trail that's been worn from use over the years. But it doesn't look like it's used often," Sparkles answered.

"And it isn't going to be easy," Grace chimed in.

"I don't think any of this is going to be easy," Liv answered. "But we don't have much time, so we'd better get going."

Liv and Moonbeam followed Sparkles and Grace on foot for a while until they arrived at the start of the trail they had described. Liv understood what they meant by "sort of a path." It was a faintly worn trail that zigzagged its way up the side of a

mountain until Liv could no longer see where it went. It either wrapped around the mountain to start going to the other side or was covered in snow. From where they were, Liv couldn't tell.

"Let's do it," Liv said. She kind of felt like they were charging head on into something without thinking about it much like Ava would, but she didn't have a lot of time, which left her with no choice. Moonbeam took the first step onto the trail, and they were on their way up.

At the bottom, the trail was very rocky. The rocks were loose, and every now and then they broke away, causing Moonbeam and Sparkles to slip. The unicorns were doing an excellent job of staying as steady as they could on the unsafe mountainside. They reacted quickly and never fell, even though it was hard to get a good footing.

As they continued working their way up, Liv could feel the temperature changing. It was getting cold. She reached into her SUSK and pulled out a hooded sweatshirt she had packed just in case it got chilly. She felt a sense of relief and immediately started to warm up when she pulled it on. She had brought this sweatshirt with her to the Unicorn Kingdom dozens of times and had never needed it. Liv thought about what her dad had taught her—"It's better to have it and not need it than need it and not have it." She thought about that often, and that's why she was always so well prepared.

Grace, on the other hand, hadn't packed anything extra. She was already shivering, and they hadn't even reached the snowy part yet. The higher up they got, the colder it felt, and the more annoying the loose rocks became. The unicorns held steady and kept them safe, but as they got higher, the rocks were tumbling farther and farther down the mountainside. It was like a constant reminder every few minutes that they were higher up and had even farther to fall.

Moonbeam and Sparkles were doing an amazing job. Liv was glad they were all able to ride on the backs of their unicorns. This hike would have been exhausting if the girls had walked up it alone. Fortunately, the trail led them between two very tall peaks so they didn't actually need to climb all the way to the top.

The sun was starting to set. It was cold and snowy where they were. Being up so high and looking down over the landscape as the sun painted the sky was one of the most beautiful views Liv had ever seen.

"It would be pretty if it wasn't crawling with vampires," Sparkles said, reminding Liv that they needed to keep their guard up.

"I think it's pretty even though it isn't perfect," Liv replied.

That caught Grace off guard since Liv was normally such a perfectionist. It made her smile, and for a moment she forgot how cold she was. The wind started to howl, and Liv pulled her sweatshirt's hood over her head. It wasn't snowing, but the wind was blowing so hard that it was whipping snow around. Liv hadn't realized how much of it had gotten stuck in her hair. As the hood started to warm her head, she felt the icy drips of melting snow drop down her neck and back.

"We aren't going to make it all the way there tonight," Liv said. "We need to find somewhere warmer to rest until morning. This hike is way too dangerous to do in the dark."

They agreed to have Sparkles fly ahead and see if she could find a safe place to spend the night. Grace was too cold to be flown through the freezing air again, so she stayed back with Liv and Moonbeam. Within a few minutes, Sparkles returned and told them she had found a small cave they could stay in to keep them out of the wind.

Sparkles led the way. Liv felt optimistic. The place Sparkles found was a perfect place for them to crash. The cave overlooked the beautiful landscape in the direction the sun was setting. In the distance they could see the black spires on the tall buildings of the Goblin Kingdom. Liv knew that somewhere below, Gork and his troll army were probably wandering around as vampires.

At the mouth of the cave was a dead tree that was broken and folded over. Liv guessed that the wind had probably knocked it down at some point. She broke off a bunch of small branches and used some matches from her SUSK to start a small fire at the mouth of the cave. She hoped the smoke wouldn't come into their cave.

It felt amazing to get out of the biting wind and into a safe place by a warm fire. They watched the sunset. Darkness set in, and far below, Liv saw purple lights at the base of the mountain.

As the night got darker, the purple lights got easier to see. It seemed like there were hundreds, maybe thousands, of them moving around at the base of the mountain. Even though they were far away, Liv was sure she saw some purple lights wandering about the Goblin Kingdom as well.

"Vampires," Grace stated.

Liv was afraid that was the case, but knowing that Grace thought the same thing confirmed her suspicion. The purple lights wandering around beneath them were the glowing purple eyes of vampires—most likely those goblins and trolls that were turned the last time they were there.

"How in the world are we going to get past all of them?" Liv wondered out loud.

"That's why we were sent here. You two will be invisible, and we'll be out of reach in the sky," Sparkles said.

Liv noticed her hands starting to get a little sweaty. "I just hope we can make it in and out fast enough."

Like always, Liv had some trouble falling asleep that night. She wished she could have blamed her restlessness on the fact that she was sleeping on a rocky cave floor. *Hopefully, there aren't too many vampires between Reagan and everyone else,* she thought to herself.

CHAPTER 4

BAD ADVICE, LIV

Ava was getting frustrated with how slowly they were moving. It was hard to move fast with such a large group. Things seemed even slower because she was used to taking advantage of Brooke's power of speed. All Ava could do to Brooke as they walked slowly, waiting for everyone else to catch up.

Claire, King Andrew, Neon, a few hundred unicorns, and every elf that had retreated to the Unicorn Kingdom were making their way back to the Elven Kingdom. Most of the elves had jumped on the backs of unicorns, but there weren't enough unicorns for every elf so some had to walk, and that is what was slowing them down.

Bram, the King of the Elves, was actually in the back walking with Goltry and the others who didn't have a unicorn to ride.

"We need to speed up," Ava said to King Andrew.

Claire, who was on King Andrew's back, answered for him. "You know how Liv always says you're charging into things without thinking everything through? I think this might be one of those times."

"We'll get there when we get there," King Andrew said. "We need to focus on being quiet, not fast. If we don't have the element of surprise on our side, we don't stand a chance."

Ava rolled her eyes but kept quiet as they slowly continued to make their way to the Elven Kingdom. They had to find a way to get the orb they needed from Reagan without hurting her or George the Dragon. They didn't want anyone on their side being bitten and turned into a vampire.

The makeshift army continued to slowly make its way through the woods. They eventually got to a point where King Andrew stopped all of them. He waited for everyone to get caught up and then started to have a conversation with Bram.

"I don't think we should get any closer until we're ready to strike," King Andrew whispered to Bram.

Bram nodded and whispered back, "I agree. I can send in some scouts to see what we can learn to help us with our attack." He turned to Goltry and said, "Bring three scouts with you. See how close you can get. Try to locate the orb so we can build a plan."

Ava interrupted. "We need to get inside and check on the Historian."

"What?" Bram exclaimed. "That place is likely to be crawling with vampires. Unless you want to turn into one yourself, you need to stay far away from there."

Ava shook her head. "I promised Liv we would check on him. We're going in, and you can come if you want."

Claire looked at Ava nervously. "You never learn, do you?"

"We promised," Ava replied.

Goltry shook his head, showing that he didn't agree. He motioned to three elves nearby, and they walked over to him. "We are going in to check on the Historian with Ava and Claire," he told his scouts. "We are going to need to be quick and quiet."

The three elves nodded, and Ava hopped off the back of Brooke.

"You don't honestly think I'm not coming with you, do you?" Brooke asked.

"Your hooves are going to be too loud. We'll get caught for sure if you come," Ava replied.

"If you get caught, I could just outrun the vampires and save you," Brooke said.

"We won't get caught," Claire said confidently as she climbed down off of King Andrew.

"We don't know this land like you do," Ava told Goltry. "You guys lead the way, and we'll make sure we keep up."

"I will lead the way," Goltry stated, "but we need you to understand our hand signals so we can communicate without talking. When I raise my fist up next to my head, that means stop. You don't start moving again until I start moving."

"Got it," Ava said. "Let's go."

Goltry and his three scout elves began walking through the woods toward the Elven Kingdom. It was the dead of night, but luckily the moon was shining so brightly that Ava could see at least a few feet ahead. As they were walking, they heard a large, cracking sound from behind them. Goltry's fist immediately shot up, and everyone came to a halt. He looked back and saw Ava standing on a broken stick. He silently made his way back to Ava and Claire and whispered, "Unless you want to join Reagan and George the Dragon as vampires, you'd better watch your step."

Ava and Claire nodded. Goltry walked back to the front and started leading them again. They slowly and silently crept through the woods until they got to a clearing where they could see the dark outline of the structures in the Elven Kingdom. Goltry sat for a few moments, staring intently and searching for any signs of vampires. He didn't see any, so he tapped the shoulder of one of his soldiers and pointed to the closest structure. The scout quickly and quietly sprinted to the building. The coast was clear, so Goltry got up and ran to the structure. Everyone else followed.

Goltry inched his way to the corner of the structure. The rest of them quietly shuffled their feet to stay close. As soon as Goltry got to the corner and poked his head around, his fist shot up in the air again, and everyone stood perfectly still. He crouched down, and the others did the same. He quickly led them behind some nearby boulders to hide.

They heard footsteps coming. The feet sounded heavy, but it was tough to hear them over the snarling sounds they heard. They stayed low and saw an elf walk by with glowing purple eyes and fangs poking out from his upper lip. It kept growling and snarling as it walked by, but thankfully it didn't see them.

As soon as the elf was far enough away to safely move, Goltry led the way again. They kept moving as quickly and silently as they could from structure to structure. They made their way up the switchback that leads to the library where they hoped to find the Historian.

They continued making their way toward the library. Goltry was taking them on the most direct route possible when they went around a corner to head to the next structure. His fist shot into the air again.

Why are we stopping in the open? We're sitting ducks here! Ava thought to herself. Then she heard a loud noise to her right that caught her so off guard that she had to cover her mouth so she wouldn't let out a scream. The loud noise she heard right next to her was breath exhaling from a vampire dragon's nose. George the Dragon was asleep a few feet away from them with vampire Reagan sleeping on his back.

Goltry slowly took a step back, and everyone else did the same. They backpedaled until they got back to the previous structure. Goltry took a deep breath and started quietly taking a different route. Ava wondered if she should just try to get the orb from Reagan now while she was sleeping. But she didn't have a way to communicate that to Goltry, and she didn't dare talk. She continued to trust and follow his lead.

Goltry led them around another way that took a little longer. Ava was glad he knew his way around this place so well. She was also glad they hadn't woken up George the Dragon or Reagan a few minutes earlier. Goltry poked his head around another corner and looked to see if the coast was clear. He tapped a scout on the shoulder and pointed toward a tall building straight ahead. The scout quietly made his way over to the structure.

Goltry walked back to Ava and spoke for the first time. He quietly whispered, "He made it. Let's head over there and check it out. Hopefully, the Historian is still there and safe." Goltry then began walking to the corner and looked again. He tiptoed quietly toward the library. As soon as the other two elves, Ava, and Claire, made it around the corner and were out in the open, Goltry's fist shot up in the air again. Everyone stopped.

Goltry quickly hit the deck and lay flat on his stomach. The rest of them did the same.

It was dark, but Ava could see a set of purple eyes walking around the corner of the library that Goltry's scout was standing in front of. By the time the scout noticed the vampire lurking nearby, it was too late. The scout elf started to sprint away. The vampire immediately turned its head, snarled, and chased after him.

"No, please!" the elf yelled as he ran. Even though the elf had a head start, the vampire quickly closed the gap. Apparently when the elf shouted, it alerted other vampires because suddenly the place was swarming with glowing purple eyes chasing after the lone elf.

"Now is our chance!" Goltry said. He pushed himself off the ground and sprinted across to the library. The remaining two scouts, Claire, and Ava followed. Just as they opened the door, they saw the lone elf running, but then a vampire tackled him to the ground and bit him.

Before they could see anything else, Goltry opened the door, pushed them all inside, and shut the door behind them.

"We need to do something! We need to help him!" Ava whisper-yelled.

"There is nothing we can do for him now except get this orb so you can defeat Luca," Goltry said. "It cost me a scout, but I got you here. I hope you're happy. And I hope that if the Historian is still alive, he will be able to help us somehow. Otherwise, my elf was just turned into a vampire for nothing."

"I hope so too." Ava said. *Coming here was bad advice, Liv,* she thought to herself.

Everyone quietly walked inside to see if they could find the Historian. It wasn't long before they saw the cloaked figure holding his lantern and walking around the library alone. When he heard them, his head shot up. Ava had never been more grateful to see normal eyes that weren't glowing purple.

He stared at them for a moment and then shrugged his shoulders and said, "I thought if I ever saw any of you again that Liv would've been the one to come here."

"We're here because we promised her we'd check on you," Ava told him. "She was worried something happened to you. We came here to make sure you're okay and to save you."

The Historian shook his head. "I swore an oath. No Historian has ever abandoned their job, and I do not intend to be the first to leave."

"We risked our lives to come here," Ava said, sounding frustrated.

"I never asked you to," the Historian said. "I don't need your help. I am glad you're here, though, because I want to help you."

Ava took a breath, glad they hadn't lost one of Goltry's soldiers to the vampire hoard for nothing.

"Help us how?" Claire asked the Historian.

"I found out why dragons and vampires have returned to our world," he replied.

Claire raised her eyebrows in surprise, "Why is that?"

"It's because of you," he said, pointing at Ava and then at Claire.

"What? That doesn't make any sense," Ava answered.

"It makes perfect sense. I can't say exactly how or why, but somehow humans throw our world off balance. For some reason, whenever you show up here, bad things happen. I fear it is happening because you don't belong here."

Ava shook her head, refusing to accept this. "But we didn't do anything wrong."

"Unfortunately, just your presence seems to be enough to open up doors to the darkest parts of this world. Think about it. Grace came here first, and Neon took over and ruined the Unicorn Kingdom. Then you all showed up, and a dragon appeared for the first time in hundreds of years. You continue to come, and Luca returns. These are connected somehow. It isn't a coincidence."

"So we should leave?" Claire asked, sounding confused.

"Not until you fix what you've started. Simply leaving won't make Luca go away. You'll need to solve that before you go."

"And once we get rid of Luca and save the world, we can't come back ever again?" Ava asked.

The Historian hung his head, and then with his nose still facing the ground, he looked up at Ava and replied, "I'm afraid so."

"How does that help us?" Ava shrieked. "We love it here."

"That doesn't help you—that helps the rest of us," the Historian said. "Ever since the vampire dragon showed up here, I've been researching a way to defeat it, and I think I have the answer." He reached into his cloak and pulled out a small vial of what looked like a thick, silver liquid.

"From everything I've read," the Historian told everyone, "this potion will put a dragon to sleep for a few hours."

"Will it work on a vampire dragon?" Ava asked.

"I hope so," he said.

"Me too," Ava quickly agreed. "What are we supposed to do, just politely ask George the Dragon to drink this and put himself to sleep for a while?"

The Historian handed the vial to Ava. "I would recommend putting the potion on the tip of an arrow and firing it at the dragon."

"Won't that hurt him?" Ava asked.

"It shouldn't. If you can actually manage to hit him, it'll feel more like getting pricked with a needle," the Historian explained. "There isn't much in the vial. I would guess that you have enough for two shots. If you can hit the dragon with the first shot, I would recommend using the second arrow on the girl who rides on the dragon's back."

"That's not an option," Ava replied. "Getting nailed with an arrow might not be a big problem for George, but we definitely can't use an arrow on Reagan. She's our friend, and it isn't her fault that she's a vampire."

"Suit yourself. Then perhaps you could politely ask your friend to drink it," the Historian said sarcastically.

Ava nodded. "We'll figure it out from here. Thanks for all your help. Are you sure you don't want to come with us?"

"Thank you, but I will not be leaving the library. I'll be here keeping track of what happens and making sure it's written down as part of our history. We're all counting on you. Good luck."

With that, Goltry opened the door, and they crept back outside into the darkness of the night. They slowly made their way back to the woods. They made it safely, and Ava was grateful their trip back was uneventful.

Once they arrived, Neon was the first to notice them and ask where the third elf scout was. Goltry shook his head sadly. "He's part of the vampire army now."

King Andrew and Bram were now nearby, and Ava explained to the two kings that they had a potion to put George to sleep. They just had to put it on an arrow and hit George to knock him out.

"We're in a better place than we were earlier. Good work," King Andrew said.

Bram stepped forward with a quiver on his back and a bow in his hand. "I'll fire the arrow."

Ava was glad they at least had a way to knock George the Dragon out of the fight. She still didn't have an answer for how they were going to get the orb from Reagan, and that made her nervous. Despite everything that was going on, right now she was most upset with the thought of never being able to come back to the Unicorn Kingdom after they saved it.

CHAPTER 5

THE PINK ORB

The next morning when Liv and Grace woke up, they looked out over the edge of the mountain where they had seen all the glowing, purple eyes the night before. They could still see movement below, but it looked like there were not nearly as many vampires around this morning as there were last night.

Finally, a little bit of luck, Liv thought to herself.

"What would you think if Sparkles and I flew overhead to see if we can locate the orb?" Grace asked Liv.

Liv bit her lip, thinking hard before she answered. "That sounds like it would be safe. Moonbeam and I will make our way down the mountain until we need to disappear."

"Then I'll turn us invisible and get us to the front gate of the Goblin Kingdom," Moonbeam chimed in.

Grace nodded. "Perfect. We'll circle above and see if we can find where they're hiding that thing. We'll meet you near the gate and decide what to do next."

Grace hopped on Sparkles' back, and they took off to begin their search.

Liv jumped onto Moonbeam, and they continued to make their way down the mountainside. As they got lower and the snow thinned out, it was easier to see a path, which helped them travel safely and quietly.

Once they were about three-quarters of the way down, Liv decided it was time to play it safe. "I think it's time to hide," she told Moonbeam.

Without saying a word, Moonbeam turned on her power of invisibility. Liv could feel her unicorn beneath her, but she couldn't see her trusted friend or herself. Completely invisible, they made their way down the rest of the mountainside.

When they reached the bottom, it started to get scary. There were vampire trolls wandering around. Liv had always thought trolls were a bit terrifying, considering they are monsters and all, but when they were turned into vampires, they were even more frightening.

Their blue skin and bodies didn't look any different than normal, although Liv did notice that they seemed more fit than before. She remembered trolls being a little pudgy, but these seemed like they either exercised a lot, didn't eat much, or both.

Moonbeam carefully navigated her way through the vampire trolls. Every now and then, Liv saw a set of purple eyes looking their way. She was afraid one of them might hear them or smell them. Moonbeam would hold still, and Liv would hold her breath until the creature snarled and clicked its sharp vampire teeth and then continued to wander around.

Liv couldn't help but feel like she was surrounded by a bunch of zombies. They seemed to wander around stupidly. But she knew that once they found something they wanted to turn into a vampire, it was like a switch flipped, and they became ferocious, quick hunters.

As Moonbeam and Liv continued to make their way through the small swarm of vampires, they stumbled across a vampire that looked strangely familiar. It hobbled by, snarling. Its purple eyes seemed to be staring off into space as he practically limped instead of walked. It was Gork—Vampire Gork. Liv had to point her eyes upward and blink away the tears when she saw the troll.

He had saved her life the last time she was there. Now he was stumbling around—a reminder of the price he had paid so Liv could escape.

Moonbeam kept walking, which helped Liv focus on her mission. It was good to remember why she was risking so much.

Get the orb. Defeat Luca. Save the world. Liv kept repeating that over and over in her head as Moonbeam made her way to the Goblin Kingdom. If she did her job and they had just a little bit of luck, it wouldn't be long before Gork would be free of the vampire magic that had turned him into a dangerous monster.

Before long they were clear of any vampires they could see. "I think it's okay to stop using your power for now, Moonbeam. You should save your strength," Liv told her.

Instantly they were visible again. Not being surrounded by vampires allowed Moonbeam to pick up the pace. Within minutes they were approaching the gate of the Goblin Kingdom.

Liv could feel her body tense up as she squeezed Moonbeam hard with her legs.

"Can't breathe," Moonbeam whispered.

"Sorry!" Liv whispered back as she loosened the grip her legs had on her friend. "I think we can stay visible, but go slowly. If anything spooks you, just turn us invisible."

Moonbeam nodded and continued forward. It seemed oddly quiet as they approached. When they got closer, Liv started to pick up on some noises—noises she *was not* happy to hear. Growling. Snarling. The sounds were low and hard to hear on the other side of the wall that surrounded the Goblin Kingdom. Liv knew it was a bunch of vampires that were just waiting to claim their next victim.

A loud thud came from behind them. Liv's heart started to flutter as fear coursed through her body. She immediately looked down and saw she was no longer visible. She was hidden, thanks to her unicorn.

Great save, Moonbeam, she thought to herself as she tried to catch her breath. Moonbeam was already on the run when Liv heard a familiar voice from behind.

"It's just us!" Sparkles said.

"You scared me half to death!" Moonbeam hollered under her breath, trying to remain quiet.

Liv looked down again and noticed she was visible. Moonbeam had turned her power off again. "I think you scared me three quarters to death. Did you find where they're keeping it?"

Grace nodded. "We did, and it's not going to be very easy to get it."

"General Gorum has it," Sparkles added.

Liv wasn't very surprised by this. "Where do we find him?"

Grace scratched her head nervously. "He's just kind of wandering around in the streets with all the other vampires. It'll be tough to get at him."

"And that's the good news," Sparkles said.

Liv started to chew her bottom lip. "If that's the good news, what is the bad news?"

"Even if you get him alone, our pink orb is now embedded into a ring on his right hand," Grace explained.

Liv put her hand over her mouth and started to think. She was normally the one who came up with the plans, but lately it seemed like there was never an answer to the situations she found herself in. She was frustrated. She hated more than anything not being able to figure out the answer to a problem. Well, actually she hated vampires more than anything, but unsolvable problems were definitely a close second.

"This is harder than trying to catch a jackalope with a butterfly net," Liv said.

Grace made a weird face at Liv. "What does that even mean? That's not a saying."

"Yes, it is. I heard my dad say it once."

"Your dad is weird."

Liv and Grace laughed.

Taking a quick breath seemed to help Liv focus better. "We need a distraction."

Sparkles stepped forward. "What do you have in mind?"

"What if Moonbeam and I sneak in and find General Gorum? Once we spot him, we can give you some kind of a signal. Then you can fly over and try to get all the other vampires to follow you while we try to get the orb."

"What will the signal be?" Grace asked.

"I'll yell 'orb' at the top of my lungs," Liv replied. "We can stay invisible so no one can see us."

"Sounds good," Grace said. "Sparkles and I will fly overhead, and when we spot General Gorum, we'll circle overhead to lead you to him. It would be tough to find him in there on your own with all those vampires wandering the streets."

Moonbeam nodded. "Let's go."

Liv jumped on Moonbeam's back, and Moonbeam turned them both invisible. They slowly made their way to the front gate of the Goblin Kingdom. The gate was still cracked open from the last time they were there. Liv looked through the opening and could see several vampire goblins wandering around the streets of what was once General Gorum's kingdom. Even though he and his goblins were still there, it was Luca's kingdom now.

Over her shoulder, Liv saw Sparkles and Grace take off and start circling overhead to wait for the signal. Moonbeam used her nose to nudge the door open. It creaked, and the vampires wandering the streets all stopped. Their heads snapped toward the door, their purple eyes staring right through Liv and her invisible unicorn.

Moonbeam held still until they eventually started wandering around again. As quietly as she could, Moonbeam continued to creep forward. Liv looked up and saw Sparkles flying around with Grace on her back. Before long they saw Sparkles quietly circling overhead a few blocks away.

Moonbeam saw that about the same time as Liv did and started making her way to General Gorum. They slowly and quietly continued to make their way there. They were getting very close. It was kind of hard to judge exactly how far away they were from Sparkles and Grace, but Liv thought they were just around the next turn from General Gorum.

Liv squeezed her legs tightly around Moonbeam as they rounded the corner and saw a sea of vampire goblins in the road. Moonbeam stopped in her tracks and slowly started to back up.

We need to find another way, Liv thought to herself. Without saying it out loud, Moonbeam also realized that was their only choice.

Instead of turning right, Moonbeam went up another block and poked her nose around the corner. She took another step out, and Liv could see the street. *All clear, thank goodness.*

Moonbeam walked down a couple more blocks as Liv tried to keep tabs on Sparkles circling above. Then Liv saw General Gorum with a pink orb mounted in a ring on his hand. On the other side of him was the sea of vampires they had almost walked into earlier. They had sneaked in behind them, and now was their chance.

Liv leaned forward so she was close to Moonbeam's ear. She whispered as quietly as she could. "You ready?"

"Do it."

"ORB!" Liv shrieked.

General Gorum's purple eyes darted to where Liv and Moonbeam were standing, but still invisible. All the vampires on the other side of the General looked toward them too. Just then, Sparkles swooped down behind General Gorum and flew straight toward the mob of vampires behind him.

They snarled and jumped at her as she flew low, but she was out of reach. The vampires turned and chased after her as she flew away. General Gorum was still staring in the direction of Liv and Moonbeam and didn't see any of this. Now was their chance.

Moonbeam started walking toward General Gorum. She positioned herself alongside him, ready to try to land a mighty kick. Just as Moonbeam was winding up, Liv heard a scream.

"You need to hurry!" Grace yelled from above.

Liv turned her head when Grace yelled. At the same time, Moonbeam started kicking, which threw Liv off balance, causing her to fall off of Moonbeam's back. The moment she wasn't touching her unicorn, she was visible. She was lying at the feet of a vampire—General Gorum.

He snarled with his fangs showing. Just as he was about to bite Liv, she heard a crunching sound, and General Gorum fell to the ground.

Moonbeam appeared next to Liv after shutting off her invisibility power. She had clearly kicked Gorum in the head just in time.

"Get that orb!" Moonbeam shouted.

Liv could hear snarling. She looked up. The mob of vampires that was following Sparkles and Grace were now charging at them.

Liv grabbed the ring on General Gorum's hand and started to pull as the unconscious vampire lay on the ground. The ring wasn't coming off.

"Hurry!" Moonbeam said as the vampires were closing in.

Liv kept pulling until the ring started to wiggle. She looked up again and saw that the vampires were practically on top of them. She pulled one last time, and the ring came off, but it was too late. The vampires were only a few feet away. She squeezed the orb with all her might and shut her eyes, ready for the mob to pile on her.

"Moonbeam, run!" Sparkles yelled.

Liv opened her eyes and saw Sparkles swooping down to her. Grace was stretching out her arm to grab Liv's hand. Without thinking, Liv instinctively reached up and felt herself being pulled off the ground by Sparkles and Grace.

She looked down and saw Moonbeam running away from dozens of angry vampires right before she turned herself invisible. With Grace on Sparkles' back and Liv hanging on, the unicorn flew out of the Goblin Kingdom. Liv was in shock as the nightmare situation disappeared from her line of sight.

CHAPTER 6

SHE'S STILL IN THERE

Ava sat on Brooke's back with the Sword of Ridder in her hand. She was ready to fight alongside the army she had brought with her.

On the edge of the forest outside the Elven Kingdom, King Andrew stood in front with Claire on his back and Neon and Bram by his side. He spoke to their army of unicorns and elves.

"Remember, we need to get Bram into range to hit George the Dragon with an arrow. Once George is asleep, this is still going to be very dangerous," King Andrew reminded everyone.

"Once George is asleep . . .," Neon started but was interrupted by Goltry.

"If the Historian's potion works," Goltry added.

"It will work," Neon responded. "And even then, getting the orb from Reagan won't be easy. She'll likely be surrounded by vampires, and it will be hard to get to her."

"Without that orb, we won't stand a chance," King Andrew reminded everyone.

Neon nodded. "Sacrifices will have to be made. If you get turned into a vampire, just remember that once we get the orb, Ava will be one step closer to being able to defeat Luca and save the world."

Everyone turned to Ava. She was so nervous that she felt like she needed to take a gulp. But she couldn't even swallow, so she simply gave a nod.

Claire could tell Ava was nervous so she spoke up for her sister. "If you get turned into a vampire, we will *never* stop trying to save you. We're going to win," she said confidently.

"Keep Bram safe so he can put George the Dragon to sleep, and protect Ava at all costs. Let's get the orb and get back home!" King Andrew shouted.

The unicorns pounded the ground with their feet in unison. STOMP! STOMP!

"Charge!" Neon ordered.

King Andrew, Claire, Neon, and Bram all turned and led the way out of the forest to the Elven Kingdom. Ava, Brooke, and their army followed.

Ahead, Ava could see hundreds of glowing purple eyes gathering together to charge back. She heard a shrill screech from above that hurt her ears and gave her goosebumps. She looked up and saw George the Dragon circling above with Reagan on his back.

The elves made their way to the front, running toward the vampires with swords drawn in one hand and a shield mounted to the other, hoping they could hold the vampires at bay. The unicorns stayed toward the back for the time being.

Hundreds of vampire elves were charging straight at them, their teeth bared and snarling like wild animals. It reminded Ava of the first time they saw Star, but she was quickly pulled back into reality when she heard King Andrew shout, "Now!"

Ava saw King Andrew's horn start to glow yellow. Behind him, hundreds of other unicorn horns started glowing yellow as well. King Andrew fired the first stun blast in the direction of the vampire mob heading their way. He hit a vampire, and it dropped to the ground. A second later, all the other unicorns behind him did the same, knocking out the first wave of charging vampires.

Ava remembered that when King Andrew first stunned Star, it wasn't long before she woke up angrier than ever. "Move quickly! They won't be down for long!" she yelled.

Everyone pushed farther forward into the Elven Kingdom. As the front line of elves with shields reached the unconscious vampires lying on the ground, they stopped.

Ava heard a screech from above. It was so loud that she had to cover her ears. George the Dragon was swooping down on the elves on the front line. He opened his mouth, and Ava was in shock as she saw the back of his mouth starting to glow purple instead of orange.

Bram was positioned well as George swooped down and began to lay down a heavy stream of what appeared to be purple fire.

Bram fired the arrow.

Ava couldn't believe how fast everything was happening. The arrow sailed through the air while many of Bram's elves were being doused in purple fire. The arrow made a direct hit into George's side. He shrieked, and the purple fire stopped as he changed course and flew back up into the sky.

As the purple fire faded, Ava was confused. She saw all the elves that she thought were on fire standing very still and not appearing to be burning at all. Then she saw them slowly start to turn around. Their eyes were purple. They had fangs. George the Dragon's purple fire was turning them into vampires.

Goltry saw this happening and yelled to his remaining soldiers. "Shift left! Protect Ava!"

Immediately and fearlessly, the remaining elves shifted and used their shields to temporarily hold back the newest set of vampires that were their friends moments before.

The vampires were so strong that they were pushing the wall of shielded elves backward. The shields were protecting them from being bitten, but Ava could see the dirt beneath their feet being pushed as they were forced back, trying desperately to hold their ground.

"Did you miss?" Goltry shouted to Bram.

"No. It doesn't seem like it worked," Bram replied.

Neon stepped up next to Bram. Ava was amazed at how calm he could still seem with all the chaos going on. "You've got one arrow left, correct? Let's hit him again. It's our only chance."

"Can you get me closer?" Bram asked Neon.

"I can if King Andrew helps clear the way."

Without giving anyone time to object, Bram gracefully swung up onto Neon's back. Neon started charging toward the shield elves who were desperately trying to hold back the mob of vampires.

"Neon, wait!" King Andrew shouted, but Neon's mind was made up. He kept charging forward toward the mob. Seeing that Neon wasn't stopping, King Andrew decided to honor what might have been Neon's final request. It was time to clear a path.

"Everyone, get ready to fire!" King Andrew shouted as he started charging in behind Neon.

All the other unicorns followed.

From King Andrew's back, Claire could see a problem as they charged. King Andrew and the other unicorn horns started glowing yellow.

"Get low!" Claire screamed at the top of her lungs.

The shield elves heard her yell and ducked as low as they could. Just then King Andrew fired a stun blast that was followed shortly by blasts from the rest of his army. Vampires were dropping to the ground like flies—at least for now.

Through all this, Neon never slowed down. He kept charging straight ahead through the sea of unconscious vampires toward George the Dragon who was swooping down at them.

"Neon, leave me!" Bram yelled. "I'm not sure if this is going to work or not, but whatever happens, you need to get Ava and everyone else out of here!"

Neon skidded to a stop and let Bram jump off. "We will never stop until we save you and everyone else," he told Bram.

"I know you won't. Now get out of here!" Bram ordered.

Neon turned and started running back toward his army. Bram stood his ground completely alone with George the Dragon flying directly at him. He pulled his last arrow with the potion on the tip from his quiver and put it in his bow. Knowing he only had one more chance, Bram pulled the drawstring back and waited. He wanted George to be as close as possible to cut down on the chances of missing him.

George's mouth started to glow purple as he flew in quickly toward Bram. As soon as George was close enough to start laying down another burst of his purple vampire fire, Bram released his arrow, aiming for George's left wing. He saw the arrow pierce the wing right before he was engulfed in purple flames.

George shrieked. His wing wasn't damaged enough where he couldn't fly, so he made a quick circle above Bram and landed next to him. Bram turned to face his former army, and Ava saw that he already had fangs and purple eyes, just like the rest of the vampires.

Bram began walking back to begin fighting his old friends. George was walking along next to him.

Ava noticed George was walking funny. His legs seemed wobbly, and his long neck and head started to droop toward the ground.

"I think it's working!" Ava shouted excitedly.

George took a few more steps and then fell over on top of Bram, pinning him to the ground. Vampire Bram growled and screeched furiously trying to get his legs out from under George's massive body, but he was stuck.

Suddenly, Ava saw Reagan pop up from behind George. Her purple eyes seemed to be staring across the battlefield right at Ava. At first, Reagan walked slowly. With every step, she picked up the pace until she was at an all-out sprint, running right for Ava.

As Reagan ran, Ava could see the purple orb they had come for in her friend's left hand. Then Ava noticed that the first wave of vampires they had stunned were starting to wake up. Some were joining Reagan in her charge.

"Brooke, you need to take me to the fight!" Ava yelled.

"I can't. It's too dangerous!"

Ava jumped off of Brooke's back with the Sword of Ridder in her hand and began running toward the charging vampires.

"No, Ava!" Claire yelled. "You're doing that thing again!"

The shield elves once again met the vampire mob with a massive force, stopping them in their tracks. The second mob of vampires lying on the ground from the most recent stun blast woke up and started joining the push.

Reagan ran up the backs of some of her vampires that were held up by the shield elves and jumped over everyone, landing behind them. All this happened right when Ava arrived. She was standing face to face with her old friend Reagan who stared back at her with glowing purple eyes and scary fangs.

Ava glanced down and saw once again the purple orb she needed in her friend's left hand. She was so close to being able to save her, but she needed to find a way to get that orb without hurting her friend.

"Reagan," Ava said as she lowered the Sword of Ridder. "I know you're still in there, and I am going to help you."

Reagan snarled and jumped onto Ava, knocking her to the ground. Reagan screeched and opened her mouth getting ready to bite, when Ava heard two loud howls come from behind her as she lay on the ground. Werewolf Mason and Leo both pounced on Reagan, knocking her off of Ava.

Goltry rushed over and tried to hold Reagan to the ground. Even though Goltry was twice the size of Reagan who was on her back, Reagan was able to throw Goltry off with ease. She stood back and began walking toward Ava again.

This time Ava raised the Sword of Ridder. When she did that, Reagan hissed at her and seemed to be afraid.

"I'm not going to hurt you, Reagan," Ava told her. "I want to help you, but I need you to give me the orb. I need you to trust me like you used to."

Reagan stayed still for a moment. Ava noticed the glow of her eyes start to fade. Then Reagan started screaming. The scream sounded like Reagan's normal voice for the first time since Ava had been there.

"Ava, I need you to help me!" Reagan yelled. Then Reagan dropped the orb on the ground and started to run away.

"Reagan, wait!" Ava yelled.

Reagan stopped and turned around. But then her eyes started glowing intensely purple again. She started to snarl and charge back at Ava.

Werewolf Mason picked up the purple orb off the ground and threw it toward Ava. Like the other orbs, when this one got close to the Sword of Ridder, it started to float and then embedded itself in the sword's hilt.

Once the orb was locked in place, Reagan and all the other vampires stopped in their tracks for a moment. None of them moved. Ava heard George roar. He woke up and got off of Bram. Reagan turned, ran back to George, and jumped on his back. Then they started to fly away.

Bram and all the other vampires followed on foot and started running in the direction that George the Dragon and Reagan were heading.

"What's happening?" Claire asked.

"They're retreating," King Andrew responded.

As all the vampires ran away, Neon figured out what was going on. "They're heading back to the Dwarven Kingdom," he said. "It's time to get home and figure out how we're going to end this thing."

Ava was still in shock that she was able to talk to Reagan for a few seconds. She was so glad her friend was still in there somewhere, and she couldn't wait to tell Liv. Then she remembered that her sister was on the other side of their secret world in a fight of her own. She hoped she'd see her back at the Unicorn Kingdom with the fourth orb.

Finally, Ava turned her focus back to her brother, Mason, and her dog, Leo. Mason had turned back into human form. Ava walked over and stared Leo down.

"Leo, it was your job to keep Mason safe. You promised you would stay away from here. Promised with an *R*," Ava scolded her dog.

Leo and Mason were standing next to each other, both looking at the ground feeling like they had done something wrong. Ava walked over, knelt down, and embraced them in a hug.

"Thank you," she whispered as Mason hugged her back and Leo's tail started wagging.

CHAPTEr 7

THE RACE

The two girls were weighing heavily on Sparkles' back. Liv still couldn't believe they had left Moonbeam behind. Sparkles flapped her wings to keep the two girls in the air safe from harm. Liv noticed the glowing, purple eyes down below starting to move.

The girls and Sparkles were in the air approaching the Troll Camp where they had seen Gork and his trolls earlier. The vampire trolls were all sprinting away from their home.

"What is going on down there?" Liv asked Grace.

"I have no idea," Grace responded. "I wonder where they're going."

Sparkles continued to fly, and by the time they were directly over the Troll Camp, there were no vampires left. They had vanished.

"I can't fly the two of you much longer. It looks safe down there now, so I am going to land," Sparkles told the girls.

Once they got on the ground, Liv saw all the footprints heading in the same direction.

"Where do you think they're going?" Liv asked.

Sparkles took a long look at the way the tracks were going. "That direction only leads to one of two places. They're heading either to the Unicorn Kingdom or the Dwarven Kingdom."

"Those things are really fast. If they're heading that way, do you think we could beat them back?" Liv asked.

Sparkles made a face like she was thinking hard. "You two are heavy. I'll try to fly us over the mountain, but once we get to the other side, we're going to need to go on foot."

Liv and Grace jumped back on top of Sparkles, and she took off toward the mountain. It wasn't long before they were flying over the top and heading back down the other side.

"You two can stay on my back, but I need to walk now," she said once she landed.

Within a few hours, Liv, Grace, and Sparkles arrived back at the Unicorn Kingdom where they anxiously waited for everyone else to return.

When the sun started to go down on the horizon, Grace spotted the army that was returning from the Elven Kingdom. "Look! There they are!" she shouted happily.

Liv was searching frantically trying to make out if her sisters were there or not. She was happy to see they were returning but couldn't help noticing that the army was much smaller than when it left. She had a sick feeling in her tummy knowing that everyone didn't make it back and that Luca's army of vampires had grown yet again.

"Oh my goodness," Sparkles whispered, sounding very worried.

Liv turned to her and saw Grace and her unicorn, Sparkles, staring in the opposite direction. The mob of vampires—likely trolls, goblins, and maybe even the vampire Moonbeam—were heading toward them.

"Sparkles, you need to go warn them—*now*!" Liv yelled.

Without a moment of hesitation, Sparkles took off and flew to the north toward King Andrew and the army. She flew as fast as she could, but Liv wasn't sure it was fast enough. In the distance, Liv saw Sparkles land next to King Andrew. Then all the elves started scrambling to get onto the back of a unicorn.

Brooke shot out of the army with Ava on her back, heading toward the Unicorn Kingdom like a missile and using her power of speed to outrun everyone. Sparkles followed, and then a cloud of dust appeared as King Andrew and the rest of the unicorns started running toward the Unicorn Kingdom. They hoped they could beat the vampire mob back to their home.

"We need to open the gate!" Liv shouted.

Liv and Grace sprang into action and started sprinting to the front gate to open it and let their friends inside.

By the time they got to the gate and opened it, Ava and Brooke were outside waiting. They dashed in immediately.

"Did you get it?" Liv shouted to her sister.

"We got it!"

Liv took out the pink orb she had pulled from General Gorum's hand earlier that day and tossed it to Ava. As Ava reached out to catch it, the orb stopped mid-air, floated toward the Sword of Ridder, and embedded itself in the hilt.

Four out of five, Liv thought to herself.

"Get ready to close the gate!" Sparkles yelled from above. "They're almost here!"

Liv looked up at the flying unicorn and yelled back, "Who is almost here? King Andrew or the vampires?"

Sparkles took a second to look around from above. "Both! Shut it on my command!"

King Andrew and Neon were the next two to burst through the door. Claire was on King Andrew's back. Liv was angry but not surprised to see Mason riding on Neon's back with Leo following closely behind.

"Keep moving!" King Andrew yelled as hundreds of unicorns piled in behind them. "Hold the gate open until everyone is in."

Liv was ready to release the lever that would slam the gate shut.

"You need to close it now. They're coming!" Sparkles yelled from above.

Liv looked to King Andrew.

"Not yet!" he yelled to Liv. "We need to save everyone we can!"

"Liv, they're coming! Shut it now!" Sparkles screamed.

"Not yet!" yelled King Andrew.

Liv stared at the door, watching the last few unicorns sprint through and hearing the snarling of vampires in the background not far behind.

"NOW!" King Andrew yelled.

Liv released the lever, and the door slammed shut just as the last unicorn and elf ran safely into the Unicorn Kingdom.

Everyone sat in silence as they heard what sounded like thousands of footsteps on the other side of the gate. The snarling was so loud that it sent chills down their spines. It continued outside for a few minutes but seemed to get quieter as they all stared intently at the door waiting for the vampires to attack.

"I think they're running away!" Sparkles yelled from above.

King Andrew and Neon trotted over to Liv.

"Did you get the orb?" King Andrew asked.

Liv nodded.

"Where is Moonbeam? Is she okay?" Neon asked.

Liv looked at the ground. She hadn't had much time to process what had happened.

"We . . . got the orb, but we lost her," Liv responded.

"Lost her? What do you mean lost her?"

Liv's eyes started to water. "Sparkles flew me and Grace out, but Moonbeam was trapped in the Goblin Kingdom, surrounded by vampires. She turned invisible, but I don't know what happened to her."

Everyone jolted when they heard a loud bang outside the gate.

Neon and King Andrew immediately turned to face the noise.

There was another bang from outside. Something was pounding on the door.

"Everyone, get ready!" King Andrew yelled.

Sparkles landed and joined the rest of the unicorns. King Andrew's horn started to glow yellow. Neon's started to glow red. Many of the other unicorns around them also had their horns glowing yellow. The elves on the backs of unicorns all drew an arrow with their bows and aimed at the door.

"Open the gate, Liv," King Andrew said. "Let's get this vampire in the dungeon next to Star."

Liv pulled the lever. The gate opened, and Moonbeam stumbled in.

"Moonbeam!" Liv yelled as she sprinted over to her unicorn and gave her a huge hug.

Now that Moonbeam was safely inside, Claire jumped off King Andrew's back and closed the gate. Neon let Mason down and then trotted over.

"I was so worried about you," Neon told Moonbeam.

Neon leaned in and put his head on Moonbeam's neck. Moonbeam leaned back into Neon, cradling her chin on top of his neck.

Moonbeam's horn started to glow light blue, and Neon's started to glow red. A beam shot out of the tip of each of their horns, looping up into a curve and forming the shape of a heart above their heads. Where the blue and red magic met in the middle, it turned purple.

Neon's eyes shot open, and Moonbeam's head jerked back.

"MOONBEAM! Mom and Dad are going to freak!" Brooke yelled at her big sister.

Neon looked shocked. Moonbeam looked slightly embarrassed, and King Andrew had a giant smile on his face.

"Umm . . . anyone

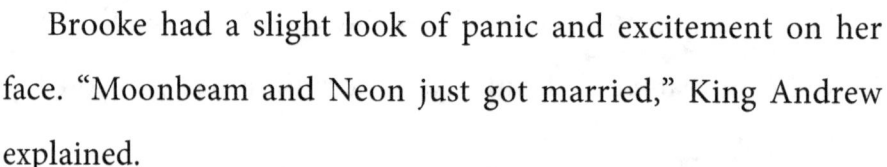

mind telling us what just happened?" Ava asked.

Brooke had a slight look of panic and excitement on her face. "Moonbeam and Neon just got married," King Andrew explained.

"WHAT?" Liv, Ava, Claire, Grace, and Leo all shouted at once with their jaws hanging open.

"Just like that? They're married? There's no party? No ceremony or anything?" Liv asked.

"You just saw the ceremony," King Andrew said excitedly.

"True. How did that even happen?" Claire asked King Andrew.

"A unicorn's heart knows what it truly loves, often before its mind does. Whether or not they knew they were meant to be and whether or not they felt ready in their minds, their hearts knew it was time. They're soulmates now!"

Liv stood there still in shock that just like that her unicorn had a husband. "You guys picked a heck of a time to get married, you know that? You couldn't have waited like two days?"

Moonbeam stared at the ground sheepishly, and Neon stood next to her proud and smiling. Liv noticed that this was the first time she had ever seen Neon smile.

"I feel like after this is all done, we need to have a real wedding," Grace said.

"I could be your maid of honor, Moonbeam," Liv said.

"What's a wedding?" King Andrew asked.

"Well, a wedding is how humans get married. There is usually a ceremony and then a huge party afterwords" Liv explained.

"What's a party?" Neon asked.

Claire shouted excitedly, "It's fun! You know, with dancing and music and cake and stuff."

"You guys are confusing me. What's a cake?" King Andrew asked.

"It's like a treat you have for dessert. There are all different kinds—chocolate, vanilla, and confetti, to name a few," Claire replied.

King Andrew's eyes lit up. "I want a Cheetos cake."

Claire giggled. "Eww."

Goltry was finally the one to reel everyone in. He cleared his throat obnoxiously to get their attention.

"Not to be rude," Goltry said, "but shouldn't we probably start figuring out how to get the last orb from Luca? If we don't find a way to get that orb back and defeat him, there isn't going to be a world left for the happy couple to enjoy."

As all this was going on, Ava didn't have the heart to tell her sister what she had learned earlier from the Historian. If there was a party here, they wouldn't be attending. Their attempt to save the world would be their final act in the Unicorn Kingdom. If the Historian was right, the only way to restore balance to this world was for them to stay away from it.

CHAPTER 8

ONE LAST PLAN

King Andrew, Neon, and Goltry stood on the throne in front of the remaining unicorns, the elves, the girls, Mason, and Leo.

Liv had learned only moments ago of Bram's heroic sacrifice. The remaining elves elected Goltry as their king until they could hopefully break the vampire curse and get Bram back.

"This is going to be the toughest situation we've faced yet," King Andrew stated. "By now, every vampire is likely back inside the Dwarven Kingdom, ready to protect Luca and the final orb."

"How will we ever get to him?" Liv asked.

"*We* don't need to get to him—*Ava* needs to get to him," King Andrew reminded everyone.

"Once we get there, the unicorns will be our best hope," Goltry stated. "We'll need all the stun power we can get. If you knock as many out as possible, we can charge in after with our shields to try to clear the way."

"There will be too many of them in there," Neon pointed out. "By now, there are probably thousands of vampires lurking inside that place. With no space, we'll just get overwhelmed."

Brooke spoke up next. "What if we lure them out? Ava and I could go in first. If they see her with the Sword of Ridder and four orbs, they'll probably chase us. I've outrun them before, and I can definitely do it again."

"That's a great idea. It is risky, but I think it's worth the risk," King Andrew said. "My biggest concern is that they know we're coming. They don't know when, but they know—and they'll be ready. How can we use the element of surprise when they're waiting for us?"

"We could put elves on the backs of the unicorns that have the power of invisibility," Goltry stated. "We could stay invisible and hide while Ava lures out as many as possible. Brooke could use her speed to run back into the cave, and we could fall in after her and block the entrance. Rather than waste stun power to defeat them, we could just box them out of their own kingdom. We could hold them out as long as we can at the entrance while you guys finish up the fight inside."

"But if we don't get the orb or if something goes wrong, we'll be trapped," Liv pointed out.

Neon spoke up next. "We're already trapped, Liv. This is it for us." Neon looked at Goltry. "If you can hold them out, we will finish up what's left and get the orb."

His eyes turned to Ava. "We'll get you that orb, and then you can finish this."

Ava looked nervously at her sisters. *No pressure there*, she thought to herself.

King Andrew spoke up to end the conversation. "Remember, while we are going to be in a fierce fight, it is important not to hurt the vampires. It isn't their fault that they're like this, and they are our friends and family. We just need to defeat Luca, and then we'll get them all back."

"Get some rest tonight. We leave in the morning," Neon shouted.

For the first time since Liv got back to the Unicorn Kingdom, she thought of home. She did some math in her head and was surprised at how far ahead of schedule they were. If they wrapped this up tomorrow, they could be home with Mason in time for dinner back on Earth.

If they didn't, she might never see her parents again. She quickly pushed that thought away and started to think about how she could help her siblings get home safely. She walked over to her family and Grace and said, "We'd better talk."

They started walking somewhere private. On the way, Claire spotted Neon and Moonbeam walking together. Neon had a giant smile on his face. Claire thought he looked funny with a smile because he was normally so serious all the time. She decided his smile didn't look funny; she just wasn't used to it yet.

As the newlyweds rounded a corner, Claire heard Neon say to Moonbeam, "I have something important I want to talk to you about."

Claire saw her sisters walking ahead of her and thought to herself, *I'll catch up with them in a minute.* She knew she probably shouldn't listen to Neon and Moonbeam talk, but they were so cute she couldn't help it.

"You're smiling," Moonbeam told Neon.

"I know. It's weird. It's weird, and I can't stop doing it."

"It is weird, but in a good way, right?"

"Absolutely!" Neon agreed. "Look, I just have a few things I want to say to you, and I think this is why I'm smiling so much. My whole life I've felt like I have just been trying to survive. And even though tomorrow is going to be all about surviving, I can't help but feel like I'm actually here to *live* for the first time in my life."

Moonbeam looked at the ground again. "That's really sweet and actually kind of sad. I'm happy too. And I'm happy you're happy. I'm just sorry it took you this long to feel happiness."

"You make me a better unicorn. And you make me *want* to be a better unicorn. Once we win this tomorrow—and we *will* win this—I am really looking forward to spending the rest of my life with you, trying to make you feel as happy as I feel."

Claire giggled and tried to catch up with her sisters. *They're just too cute*, she thought to herself.

After a few minutes, she caught up with her sisters.

"Ugh. I'm so nervous," Ava said. "I'm nervous and excited, and I feel like I'm going to puke."

Liv giggled.

"Why is that funny to you?" Ava asked.

"That's the same way I feel when I'm about to perform my dance solo. It just seems silly that we feel the same way when what you're doing is so much more important. The good news is that even though I always feel that way, I stay focused and nail it!"

"You've got this, Ava," Grace said.

As Claire walked in and sat down, she said, "We'll be there with you. We will make sure you have all the help you need."

Ava looked at the Sword of Ridder. "I wish it didn't have to be me."

Liv walked over and tried to pick up the sword, but she couldn't get it to budge. Claire and Grace tried, too, but they couldn't move it an inch. Ava reached over with one hand and picked it up with ease like she always did. "I just don't get it," she said.

She decided right then and there that it was time to start being brave. She had some tough news to share with everyone and figured now was as good a time as any.

"Liv, I forgot to tell you that the Historian is fine. He actually gave us a potion that put George the Dragon to sleep. If we hadn't checked on him, we never would've been able to get the orb from Reagan. And when I saw Reagan, for a second, she was herself. It was like she could remember me."

"That's amazing!" Liv replied.

"Did she say anything?" Claire asked.

Ava gulped nervously, trying to recall what had happened, but it had all happened so fast. "Reagan screamed. I can tell she doesn't like being a vampire."

"Can't say I blame her there," Liv stated.

"She also begged for help," Ava added.

Liv bit her lower lip like she does when she gets nervous and doesn't know exactly what to say. "We're going to help her, Ava. Tomorrow."

"There's another thing," Ava started.

Everyone could tell she sounded really serious, and Ava felt like she had their undivided attention—even from Leo.

"The Historian thinks *we* are the reason bad stuff keeps happening here."

Liv glanced over at Grace with a puzzled look on her face.

"That doesn't make any sense," Grace said.

"I know, I know." Ava replied. "It's just that . . . he seems to think we throw this world off balance somehow and that it's causing weird and bad things to happen. Grace came here long ago, and Neon took over the Unicorn Kingdom. Then we all came back, and a dragon appears."

"Yeah, but George is nice! Or . . . he was nice before the vampire thing," Claire answered.

"But before Neon wiped out his memory and Reagan trained him, he wasn't. And then we keep coming back, and now there are vampires. Maybe there is a portal or gate that's opening when we visit. Whatever it is, the Historian thinks we make this place unsafe. If we can save the world . . ."

". . . *When* we save the world," Liv corrected her sister.

"Right. When we save the world, he thinks it's best if we don't come back here anymore," Ava sadly told everyone.

Being reminded of this just about broke Claire's heart, but she had been seeing everyone else act so bravely that she decided it was her turn. "If that's what keeps everyone safest, then that's what we have to do. Did he say anything about unicorns not being able to come and visit us?"

Ava smiled. "Actually, no, he didn't."

"So we can't see them whenever we want, but we will still see them," Claire said. "Everything is going to be okay."

Once they wrapped up their conversation, everyone went to sleep.

As usual, Mason was the first one awake the next morning. He woke Liv up just as the sun was starting to light up the pink Unicorn Kingdom sky.

"Oh my gosh! What happened to you? You're filthy," Liv told her little brother.

"Vampires! Danger!" Mason shouted.

"Let's at least get you in something clean," she said as she pulled off his completely disgusting AC/DC shirt.

She reached into her SUSK and found a spare shirt she had packed. It was a blue, sleeveless T-shirt with white lettering on the front that said, "Suns out, Guns out."

Liv couldn't help but see the humor in that. "Fitting," she told her little brother. "You're coming with us today. More vampires. More danger. I'm going to need you to stay close and stay safe. We'll probably even need you to go into werewolf mode."

Mason let out a howl that woke up the rest of the girls.

Grace rolled over, half asleep, and said, "Raised by wolves."

Everyone laughed, and then they heard an elven war horn blow.

Ava picked up the Sword of Ridder. "Time to go. Let's do this," she said.

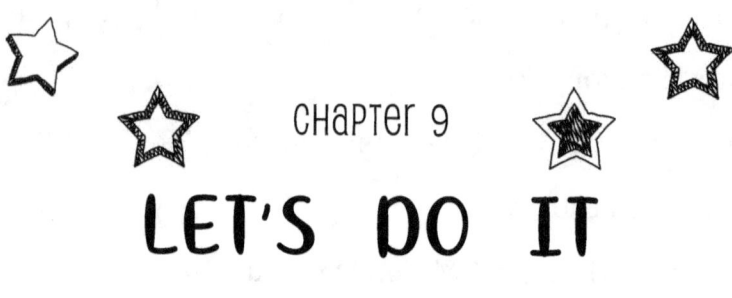

CHAPTER 9

LET'S DO IT

The last time they walked to the Dwarven Kingdom, it felt like it took forever. This time, since Liv was dreading their arrival so much, she thought the trip was over in the blink of an eye. She wished it had taken longer. They had a good plan, but she felt very nervous.

She was tense and worried about everything, like normal, but this time she was especially concerned for her sister Ava.

Liv sat on Moonbeam's back at the base of the mountain looking ahead to the entrance of the Dwarven Kingdom. She took a moment to look around and see the size of the army her group had brought along. Four young girls. A dog. A werewolf brother. All the remaining unicorns and elves that hadn't been turned into vampires yet.

Liv remembered the Historian and the mermaids that Ava had told her about. As far as she knew, that was everyone left in the world. She thought about all her friends who had been turned into vampires.

Reagan. George the Dragon. Gork. General Gorum. Star. Bram. The list went on and on. So many were taken before they even knew what they were really dealing with. Once they found out what was going on, many had heroically sacrificed themselves so Liv could stand in this very position with the army surrounding her.

We're coming, Reagan. We're going to save you. We're going to save everyone, Liv thought to herself.

Liv glanced to her right and looked at Ava. She knew her sister was terrified, but she was doing a good job of not showing it.

"Whatever happens, we're in this together, Ava," Liv told her sister.

King Andrew walked up at that moment, and Claire chimed in. "We've got your back, no matter what."

Ava nodded and pulled out the Sword of Ridder.

King Andrew and Neon walked to the front line with Claire and Mason riding on their backs.

"Remember the plan!" King Andrew yelled. "Elves on the backs of unicorns with the power of invisibility! Brooke will lure them out. Once we've got as many out as possible, we will sneak in with Leo and the humans, and it's your job to seal them off."

Neon stepped forward. "Invisibility unicorns. Help the elves hold their ground. What we need more than anything is time."

"Stunners will be with me," King Andrew said. "We will try to knock down anything between us and Luca. Once the path is clear, we need to get the orb to Ava."

"Ava, once you have the last orb, finish him off once and for all," Neon told her. "We will all be there with you the entire time, and we'll do whatever we can to help."

"You ready, Sis?" Claire asked.

"Ready as I'll ever be. Let's do it," Ava replied.

Brooke took off trotting toward the opening in the mountainside that led to the Dwarven Kingdom.

It was oddly quiet as she approached. Liv didn't hear any noise at all. No snarling. No screeching. No hissing. She was glad she couldn't see any purple eyes. She expected there to be countless vampires around them, but it was so quiet that she could hear Brooke's hooves clapping against the ground as she made her way into the tunnel and out of sight.

"The Sword of Ridder with four orbs is sure to get their attention," Neon reassured everyone.

"Remember, as far as we know; we are the only creatures here that aren't vampires, other than maybe the mermaids. Everyone else is probably in there. There are going to be thousands of them," King Andrew pointed out.

It was quiet for a little while longer. Liv always hated that. Whenever they were in these situations, time seemed to go by very slowly. Every second that ticked by felt like an eternity.

Suddenly they heard a deafening screech come from inside the Dwarven Kingdom. The screech kept getting louder and louder. The entire entrance to the Dwarven Kingdom started to glow purple as Liv saw Brooke shoot out with Ava still riding on her back.

Liv finally took a deep breath after seeing that Brooke and her sister were safe.

The purple glow coming from inside the grand entrance to the Dwarven Kingdom intensified. As the glow continued to get brighter and turn a deeper shade of purple, the horrible snarling and screeching sound got even louder.

Liv started to feel the ground shake. She noticed some of the small rocks on the mountainside start to jiggle and fall. It was like a small earthquake was happening. Suddenly thousands of vampires began pouring out of the Dwarven Kingdom, chasing after Liv's little sister Ava.

It was a sea of vampires chasing after Ava and Brooke with their glowing purple eyes. Even though vampires were fast, they were no match for Brooke and Ava. Brooke kept up her super speed and led them away.

After what seemed like several thousand vampires pouring out of the cavern, the herd was finally starting to thin out. Liv had no idea how the elves were going to hold off such a massive army. She feared they weren't going to have as much time as they had hoped.

"Let's go!" King Andrew shouted as he and Neon led the way into the Dwarven Kingdom.

A few hundred unicorns with elves on their backs turned invisible. King Andrew, with Claire on his back, led the stunning unicorns into the Dwarven Kingdom, followed by Leo, Liv, Mason, and Grace, who were riding on the backs of their own unicorns.

They were in. Liv didn't see any other vampires inside. *Did Luca send them all after Ava?* she wondered.

Moonbeam stopped and turned around so she and Liv could wait for their sisters together. They saw Brooke make a wide loop, followed by thousands and thousands of vampires in the valley below. Once Brooke had the mob as far away as she could get it, she started running back to the entrance to the Dwarven Kingdom incredibly fast—even for Brooke.

As Brooke approached, the elves with shields hopped off the backs of the invisible unicorns and blocked the entrance to the cave. The unicorns became visible again and lined up behind the elves to try to hold back the mob.

Running at an incredible rate of speed, Brooke leaped into the air at the entrance of the cave and easily cleared her army that was blocking the entrance.

"Let's go!" Ava shouted as she caught back up with her friends and family.

The girls, Mason, and Leo plunged deep into the cave on the backs of their unicorns, followed by what was left of the stunners.

When they got in, they saw Luca standing next to George the Dragon with Reagan on his back.

Luca raised his hand into the air, and George started to fly up. Luca pointed toward Ava, and George started flying toward them as if Luca was controlling him.

"Hit the dragon with everything you've got!" King Andrew yelled as his horn started glowing yellow.

He fired a shot that hit George but didn't seem to slow him down much. He fired another. Then so did the other unicorns behind him. Each fired another—and another. It was actually starting to slow George down.

George shrieked, and his mouth started glowing purple. He was going down. On his way to the ground, he unleashed a wave of purple fire that hit a bunch of the unicorns that were in the back of their group. George crashed and didn't move, but the damage was done.

Dozens of the unicorns that were just helping them defeat Luca now had glowing purple eyes.

Reagan stood up on George's back, and even though her eyes were purple and lifeless, she looked furious and let out a terrifying shriek.

The vampire unicorns started charging toward the stunners. The stunning unicorns fired at them, but they didn't get them all before they started getting overrun and bitten as the few remaining members of King Andrew's army were slowly turned into vampires.

King Andrew looked to Neon. "What do we do?"

Without skipping a beat, Neon started to take the lead. Drop the humans. It's up to us now. Brooke, Sparkles—do what you can to hold them off. King Andrew and Moonbeam, we're going to get that orb from Luca *now!*

Before anyone could object, the girls and Mason were gently bucked off their unicorns. Brooke and Sparkles charged toward the vampires at the back while Moonbeam, King Andrew, and Neon all headed straight for Luca.

King Andrew was the first to get to Luca. He spun and tried to land a kick, but Luca was too fast, and he missed. He was then face to face with the vampire and launched a stun shot. Luca held up his hand and stopped it just like the last time they had met.

Next, King Andrew tried to charge with his horn. Luca took a mighty swing with his fist at King Andrew's head. Liv saw King Andrew's horn snap in half as he fell to the ground.

Everything seemed to be happening in slow motion. Liv looked behind her. She saw Sparkles and Brooke charge in and crash into the vampires coming from behind, only to be bitten and turned into vampires themselves.

Liv turned again and saw Moonbeam rush in. Right before she was about to make contact with Luca, she turned invisible. Luca raised his hand and squeezed. As he held tight, Moonbeam became visible again. Luca had her by the throat. He seemed to stare right at Ava as he bit her. Moonbeam's eyes started to change.

Ava heard a screech behind her. As she turned, she saw several unicorn vampires pin Grace and her family to the ground and bite. Even Leo was captured, and everyone's eyes started to glow purple.

As Ava's friends and family stood up with new sets of fangs and purple eyes, she heard Neon shout.

"Nooo!" he yelled as his horn flashed red so brightly that it blinded Ava.

The entire cavern was engulfed in a red blast that echoed and carried throughout the Dwarven Kingdom. Ava saw the blast coming, and it seemed to go right through her.

Whatever Neon had just done caused all the vampires and many of Ava's friends and family to drop to the ground and stop moving.

Ava had no clue what type of power Neon had just unleashed, but even Luca was knocked to the ground.

For the time being, everyone except Ava, Neon, and King Andrew was a vampire. And for the moment, it was Ava and Neon against Luca.

"What just happened?" Ava shouted to Neon.

"I don't know," Neon said as he struggled to his feet. "I've never been this angry before."

Ava heard Luca start laughing the most evil laugh she had ever heard. It was even scarier than the ones she used to hear from Neon.

Neon looked at Luca, then at Ava, and then back at Luca.

Ava could tell he was completely drained from the incredible amount of power he had just used, but she saw him charge toward Luca. Neon lowered his head, pointing his horn at his enemy.

The evil leader of the vampire army stood still until the last second. Then he stepped to the side, grabbed Neon's horn with one hand and his chin with the other and pulled. Ava heard a cracking sound, and Neon dropped to the ground.

Luca stood and stared at Ava as everyone around her was still lying on the ground.

"Finally, it's just down to you and me," Luca said.

CHAPTER 10

BACK IN BLACK

Ava looked around her and saw that everyone she cared about was on the ground. Even though she was worried about each and every one of them, she hoped they wouldn't get up because they would be a vampire ready to turn her into one next.

Luca let out another one of his evil laughs. "I'll be honest with you, little girl. You made it farther than I thought you would. I didn't expect to have to finish you off myself."

Ava didn't say a word, trying to think of what to do next. She held up the Sword of Ridder, knowing it would be her best defense. As she raised it, Luca hissed.

"Don't you understand, little girl? With every vampire created, my power grows *stronger.* I own this world now. And as long as I have this" (he pointed to the necklace around his neck that contained the fifth and final orb), "there is nothing you can do to stop me."

Ava took a deep breath.

"Now let's get this over with," Luca said.

Just then, Ava heard some rustling behind her. She turned and saw Liv starting to stand. As Liv tilted her head up, Ava saw the fangs and the glowing purple eyes that she had feared.

Luca started to laugh again.

More movement was happening around Ava. Her family was slowly starting to rise. Claire was up next. Then Mason. Then Leo. And finally her good friend Grace, all with glowing purple eyes.

Luca was bent over, laughing. "I cannot believe this. I thought I was going to have to turn you into a vampire myself. That family of yours is tough. They're the first back on their feet after whatever Neon just did. And now you're going to be turned into a vampire by your own family!"

Liv, Grace, and Leo snarled. Claire and Mason screeched as they surrounded Ava and started to close in.

Ava held the Sword of Ridder in front of her as they all started hissing. It was frightening to see her friends and family as vampires. It was especially odd hearing Leo hiss.

Ava could see they didn't like the Sword of Ridder, so she lowered it.

"You guys told me you were going to help me," Ava said.

She wasn't positive, but she *thought* everyone actually hesitated for a moment. It was almost like they were hearing her. *Maybe they're like Reagan. Maybe they're still in there somewhere*, Ava thought to herself.

"I'm not going to hurt you," Ava told them. "I love you. I need you."

At that point, her family, Leo, and Grace had come to a complete stop. Ava heard Luca laughing again behind her.

"Silly little girl. There is nothing you can do. It's over," Luca stated.

Ava turned and held up the Sword of Ridder again. "I'm not a little girl. I'm 12 years old, and I'm way more than you'll ever understand. I'm a little sister."

When she said that, Liv walked over and stood between Ava and Luca, staring down the leader of the vampires.

"I'm a big sister . . . and a dog lover."

Claire, Mason, and Leo all walked over and stood next to Liv between Ava and Luca.

"I'm a friend," Ava said as Grace walked over and joined her family.

"And I'm your worst nightmare," Ava finished.

When she said that, her vampire friends and family started charging toward Luca. He didn't seem afraid, but he did seem caught off guard.

Apparently, the only thing as strong as a vampire is another vampire. Luca swung at Liv, but she blocked his hit with her arm. Grace kicked Luca in the stomach, and he bent over for a second.

Ava realized that was the first time anyone had been able to make contact with the evil monster.

Werewolf Mason and Leo, both in vampire form, bit Luca's legs. Grace and Liv grabbed his arms and held him still for only a moment. That moment was just long enough for vampire Claire to rip the necklace off of Luca's neck. She popped it open and pulled out the last orb—the one they needed.

"Nooo!" Luca shrieked.

When he did that, the rest of the vampires started to rise to their feet.

Claire tossed the orb to Ava, who held up the Sword of Ridder. The fifth and final orb floated to the hilt and embedded itself in the sword.

How Ava felt after that was hard to describe. She felt powerful. She felt brave. She felt optimistic, almost invincible. Everything around her seemed to move in slow motion. It was not like in the past when time seemed to pass slowly because she was scared. She actually felt as if she was able to slow down time. She knew it was impossible, but it was almost like she couldn't hear anything around her. All she could hear in her head was the song her dad blared in the car to pump his kids up for sporting events—"Back in Black" by AC/DC.

She didn't feel like she was in a rush because she was able to look around and analyze her surroundings very quickly. Everyone around her seemed to be moving extremely slowly.

She turned around and saw the endless sea of vampires charging toward her.

Looks like the shield elves have been defeated, she thought. But she wasn't worried.

She turned again and saw King Andrew attempting to get back on his feet. In slow motion, she saw some sparks shoot out of his broken horn.

She saw terror in Luca's eyes.

Luca hollered loudly. In slow motion, he seemed to be overcome with rage. One by one, he tossed Liv, Mason, Claire, Grace, and Leo to the side.

Once he was free, he screeched and started charging toward Ava.

Ava looked behind her and again saw the sea of vampires approaching. Luca was charging from the front.

Ava saw Neon still lying in a heap on the ground next to where Luca was running.

With her right hand, she held the Sword of Ridder with all five orbs firmly in the hilt. She began charging toward Luca.

Ava lunged forward toward Luca in slow motion. As she got close, she raised the Sword of Ridder high above her head and swung downward with all her might.

Luca raised his hand and caught the sword, stopping the swing instantly. He started laughing again.

Suddenly, Ava noticed an intense light flooding out of Luca's hand where he was holding the sword. The light gleamed brightly. Ava continued to hold the hilt of the Sword of Ridder loaded with all five orbs as Luca grasped tightly to the blade.

They stared into each other's eyes. Luca started to yell. The brighter the light got, the louder his yelling became. It reminded Ava of being teleported by a unicorn. It eventually became so bright that she had to shut her eyes. Even with her eyelids closed, she had to turn her head to the side because the light was still too intense.

Suddenly, Ava felt the light dim. As the light burned out, Luca's yelling stopped.

Ava opened her eyes and saw a cloud of dust blowing away where Luca had been standing moments before. Everything was unfolding before Ava as if time were still slowed down.

Ava looked over to her family, Grace, and Leo. Claire's purple eyes were the first to start to fade and turn back to normal. She saw Claire take a giant breath, almost like she was breathing for the first time.

One by one, Liv, Mason, Grace, and Leo all did the same thing. They had giant smiles on their faces and started running toward Ava.

Ava dropped the Sword of Ridder on the ground and suddenly snapped back to reality. Time returned to normal. She could hear everything around her. "Back in Black" wasn't rocking her world anymore.

Leo was the only one who paused on his way to Ava. He stopped and picked up the piece of King Andrew's broken horn in his mouth.

Liv, Claire, Mason, and Grace all tackled Ava and gave her a hug. Leo followed close behind.

As Liv wrapped her sister in a hug, she squealed, "You did it!"

"*We* did it," Ava said, smiling and hugging everyone back.

At that moment, a scream from behind startled them.

"Liv!"

Everyone turned around and saw Reagan running toward them. Liv let go of her family and ran over to hug her friend for the first time in what seemed like forever.

"I was so worried about you!" Liv yelled as she hugged Reagan.

Reagan hugged her back and then pushed her away. "What the heck took you so long?" she said with a smile on her face.

Liv and Reagan giggled. "It's a long story," Liv said. "I'll fill you in later."

Liv noticed behind Reagan that every creature that had been a vampire was now back to their true form. The world was saved.

Mason let out a howl.

The first person Liv actually recognized was Bram. He clenched both his fists, thrust them into the air, and started cheering. The entire world joined in as the Dwarven Kingdom erupted with applause and shouts of joy that the battle against the vampires was over. They had won.

With a giant smile on her face, Liv turned around to take a look at Ava. *She must be so proud*, Liv thought. But Liv realized that not *everyone* in the world was cheering. Ava had knelt down next to Neon who was still lying on the ground in a heap.

Moonbeam stood over Ava and Neon with tears streaming down her face. Liv could see Moonbeam and Ava talking, but the cheering from everyone else was so loud that she couldn't hear what was being said.

Liv rushed over to Ava. When the others saw what was going on, Leo, Mason, Claire, Grace, and Reagan followed her.

"What's happening?" Liv yelled over the cheers.

Ava looked up with tears in her eyes. "He's not breathing."

Moonbeam let out a sob. Ava leaned in and put her ear to Neon's chest.

She sat back up with tears in her eyes and stammered, "His heart isn't beating. Neon is dead."

CHAPTER 11

SUSK

Hearing that Neon's heart wasn't beating got Liv's heart thumping. She could feel it beating in her chest. *No! This can't be happening,* she thought to herself as tears started filling her eyes.

They had been through so many dangerous situations and had always managed to get through them safely. Sure, they had some close calls along the way, but nothing like this.

Moonbeam sniffled. "He was just starting to become the unicorn I always knew he could be."

Liv heard heavy breathing nearby as everyone started to figure out what was going on. Then the cheering quieted down. The noise came from King Andrew who had a look of terror and panic on his face.

"Where am I? What's going on? Who are all of you?!" King Andrew yelled, his voice trembling in fear.

Claire ran over to King Andrew and put her hand on his nose.

"Shh. It's okay, Drew," she said as she gently touched his nose and rubbed the side of his face with her other hand.

King Andrew took a deep breath and began to calm down. "What is going on, Claire? Why are we here?"

"You remember me?" Claire asked with a look of shock in her eyes. "What else do you remember?"

"Um, nothing." he replied.

"You don't remember anything that happened?

King Andrew wailed. "I can't even remember why I can't remember anything!"

Liv decided she was going to let Claire deal with King Andrew at the moment. She needed to figure out how to calm Moonbeam down and get Neon out of this place. She tried to think logically and set her sad feelings aside, but she couldn't seem to shake it. She had a tummy ache.

Ava yelled and rose up from Neon's lifeless body. She stormed over to the Sword of Ridder and picked it up.

"You worthless piece of junk!" she screamed. "The great Sword of Ridder was supposed to protect us—all of us. Why didn't it work?"

Hearing the word Ridder jogged Liv's memory. She felt like she did when she woke up from having a wonderful dream but couldn't remember what it was about unless she thought really hard. It was something important hidden way back in her mind that was making her feel optimistic.

"Oh my gosh!" Liv yelled as she dropped to her knees and pulled her SUSK off her back. She heard some other unicorns panic around her as she tried to concentrate.

"Is Neon dead?" someone asked.

"What happened to King Andrew's horn? It's broken again!" someone else exclaimed.

"Who will lead us?" said someone in the back.

Liv couldn't think. "Be quiet!" she yelled. "I have an idea." Liv unzipped her SUSK and started to rifle through all her stuff. She threw out snacks, a flashlight, and extra clothes. That's when she saw her notebook smashed at the bottom of her bag. She hadn't thought about her notebook in quite some time. It had gotten crushed on their latest adventures.

Liv opened her notebook and started flipping through the pages. She was looking for the research she had done when she was with the Historian. She flattened the damaged pages as she tried to find her notes.

Then she saw it. She read through her notes quickly until she found what she was looking for—notes on when she had first learned the story of Ridder. She saw the name Trem in her notebook. *That was Ridder's name before he was brought back to life,* Liv thought to herself.

All the unicorns in the world at that time saw how devoted Trem was to trying to save the world by ridding it of vampires. Every unicorn old enough to use their power to heal used their power at the same time on Trem's lifeless body and brought him back from the dead.

Liv stood up, beaming. "We can save him!" she shouted.

Moonbeam sniffled again. "Really, Liv? How?"

"We need every unicorn with the power to heal to use it on Neon all at once!" Liv said excitedly. It worked before on Trem, and when he was brought back to life, he was known as Ridder. If it worked for him, it can work for Neon too!"

Ava stopped being angry at the Sword of Ridder long enough to point out a problem. "But all the unicorns in the world aren't here right now, Liv. Star is still in the dungeon."

"Star already used her power to heal, so I don't think she would count," Liv reminded Ava. "They have to be old enough and still have their power. Is anyone else missing?"

"No. Everyone's here," Ava said happily.

"Wait!" Claire hollered over all the excitement, still rubbing King Andrew's face. "Shouldn't someone heal King Andrew's horn first? That way we could get him fixed up, and then everyone left could heal Neon."

Liv was stumped. "That's a great idea. I don't know if that would work or not."

"We can't risk that!" Moonbeam said. "Please, if we have a chance to save Neon, we can't miss it."

"So King Andrew is supposed to just wander around aimlessly for the rest of his life?" Claire asked. "That sounds miserable for him when we might be able to save them both."

"Save who both?" Drew asked, having no idea what was going on.

Everyone ignored this for the time being.

"He may not be able to remember much, but at least he's alive," Moonbeam pointed out.

Claire looked at the ground in frustration. She knew Moonbeam was right. She just hated the idea of not being able to save both King Andrew and Neon.

Sensing Claire was upset, Drew walked over and nudged her shoulder with his nose.

"What's the matter, Claire?" he asked.

"It's just . . . it's not fair. You shouldn't be stuck like this."

"Stuck like what?"

"Just the way you are now," Claire said.

"I don't know. I seem fine," King Andrew assured her with a smile. "You're the one who seems upset. Whatever is wrong, it's going to be okay."

"You're braver than you'll ever know, Drew," Claire said, giving him a hug.

"You guys are right," Liv said. "It's too risky to try to save them both. We need to save Neon. Do it."

All the unicorns that still had their power to heal walked up to Neon. He was lying on the ground next to Moonbeam.

There were thousands of them that circled around. Liv knew that not every unicorn here still had their once-in-a-lifetime ability to heal. But as long as everyone that still had their power used it at the same time, it should work.

"When I say go," Liv said. "1, 2, 3 . . . Go!"

Every unicorn that was circled around Neon started to chant all at once.

They repeated the phrase that had become very familiar to the girls and Leo. "*Once in my life, a miracle to make, it's time now for my power to wake. For in my soul, I can feel it's time to use my power to heal."*

With so many unicorns using their power at once, the Dwarven Kingdom lit up the most beautiful shade of pink. Even though there were so many using their powers, the light was never blinding like unicorn magic sometimes was. It was simply beautiful.

One by one, pink laser-like beams shot out of their horns toward Neon. The beams held steady, all hitting him. As the beams hit Neon, his limp body started to lift into the air. Their magic was making him float back to his feet.

As their power to heal came to an end, all the beams stopped. Neon dropped back to the ground, landing on all four of his hooves. He took a huge breath the second he was back on the ground. He smiled and looked at Moonbeam.

"When I told you I was going to spend the rest of my life trying to make you as happy as you make me, I had a bit longer time in mind," Neon said. He looked around at all the unicorns surrounding him. "Thank you for giving me a second chance."

"Second chance? This is like your fifth chance!" Moonbeam exclaimed as she charged in and nuzzled Neon.

Everyone started cheering. That was when Neon noticed King Andrew and his broken horn.

"Oh, my king," Neon said, sounding sad.

Drew had no idea Neon was even talking to him.

A unicorn that Liv had seen but didn't know personally spoke up. "With King Andrew's horn broken, we should have Neon and Moonbeam lead the Unicorn Kingdom."

"What? That's crazy. I can't . . .." Neon started.

Liv interrupted him. "Neon, you are the right unicorn for the job. You've earned this."

"All hail King Neon and Queen Moonbeam!" the unicorns yelled.

STOMP! STOMP!

All the unicorns stomping in agreement told Liv it was official. Neon and Moonbeam were now the rulers of the Unicorn Kingdom, and Drew was stuck not even remembering who he was.

Everyone was cheering.

Drew smiled next to Claire. "Everyone is so happy. This is the best day *ever*!"

"It sure is, buddy," Claire lied to her unicorn.

"Wait a second," Moonbeam exclaimed. "King Andrew doesn't need to be this way forever."

Claire tilted her head to the side, puzzled by this. "What do you mean?"

"Just because there are no unicorns left with the ability to heal today doesn't mean there never will be again," Moonbeam said. "Someone just needs to have a baby! Once it gets old enough, it can heal King Andrew!"

CHAPTER 12

THE HARDEST TRIP HOME

"Where are we going?" Drew asked.

Claire was trying to be patient, but answering the same question for the 40th time was wearing her out. "You're taking us back to the Unicorn Kingdom so we can check on Star," Claire said. "Once we see her, we're going to need some unicorn magic to take us back home."

"Oh. I don't have any magic powers anymore since my horn broke."

Claire patted Drew on the head. "I know, buddy." She kept reminding herself she was lucky that he was still alive. Even though it could take years in Unicorn Kingdom time, eventually, Drew would be better.

Claire tried to keep Drew calm and on course with the rest of the unicorns heading back to the Unicorn Kingdom. They were up in the front of the pack with Brooke, Moonbeam, Neon, Sparkles, George the Dragon, and Claire's family and friends. Even Leo was doing a good job keeping up.

As Ava rode on Brooke's back, she finally felt like she had time to ask some questions. "Liv, do you remember anything when you were a vampire?"

"Kind of."

"What was it like?"

Liv paused for a moment. "I'm not sure, but I think it was like dying. Everything got kind of fuzzy, and I was mostly seeing things in shades of purple. And I was cold." Liv felt a chill go down her spine and shivered. "So cold."

"Worse than Minnesota in January?" Ava asked.

"Way worse. And I remember feeling so . . . hopeless and sad. But then I heard your voice. At least for me, hearing you talk gave me a tiny bit of hope, and I felt the smallest bit of warmth right here," Liv said as she pointed to her heart.

"Maybe the Sword of Ridder worked better than I thought," Ava responded.

CHRONICLES OF THE UNICORN KINGDOM

Liv shook her head no. "I don't think it was the sword. I think it was you."

Reagan chimed in. "The same thing happened to me. You even snapped me out of it for a few seconds."

"How did I do that?" Ava asked, puzzled.

"I'm not positive, but I think it might've been love," Reagan answered.

Ava smiled. "I like that thought. Let's go with that."

Brooke couldn't help but overhear the conversation since she was carrying Ava. "I wonder why that didn't happen to any of us unicorns?" she asked.

"I have no clue, but however it happened, I am glad it happened when it happened," Ava pointed out.

Everyone continued marching back toward the Unicorn Kingdom. It was quiet for a bit when Moonbeam spoke up. "Liv, how much time do you have until you need to be home for dinner?"

Liv thought about the time they had spent in their secret world on this adventure. Earlier that day on Earth, she had tried to convince her parents that Mason should attend a fake sleepover so they could have more time. She couldn't believe how far ahead of schedule they were.

"After we check on Star and make sure she's okay, we'll need to leave," Liv said.

"Already? I thought you still had a few days left," Moonbeam replied.

Liv and Ava exchanged a nervous glance—the type of glance sisters use to talk without actually saying any words. Liv knew that neither of them wanted to break the news to Moonbeam or Reagan—or anyone else for that matter.

Lucky for Ava, Liv knew it was her job to share bad news since she was the oldest.

"When we go back, we will leave the Sword of Ridder and all the orbs in the Unicorn Kingdom. We'll check on Star, and then we need to go home . . . forever," Liv said.

Moonbeam giggled. "What do you mean forever?"

Liv and Ava exchanged a glance again.

"Well . . ." Liv started, but then Ava interrupted her.

"When I was in the Elven Kingdom getting the orb back from Reagan, I met with the Historian," Ava told the unicorns. "He thinks that humans don't belong here, and that's why bad things keep happening to this place."

Neon snapped his head over with a shocked look on his face. Sparkles' jaw dropped. Brooke's brow furrowed. Moonbeam no longer looked to be in a giggly mood.

"What bad things?" Drew asked.

"Oh my gosh!" Reagan said while riding on the back of George the Dragon. "You mean the return of the dragon and the vampires was because of us? How?"

"I don't exactly understand it," Ava replied, "and I don't think the Historian does either. Maybe it's like a portal or a gate that opens up and lets bad things in because we aren't supposed to be here."

Neon scoffed. "It's probably just bad timing or bad luck on your part."

"Yeah, but what if it isn't? What if this stuff keeps happening because we come here?" Liv asked. "The Historian is probably the smartest person—elf—I've ever met. I hate the idea of not coming back here, but if it's what keeps this place safe, then that's what we need to do."

Just then they walked over the crest of a hill, and the Unicorn Kingdom was visible on the horizon.

"This is the most emotional day of my life!" Moonbeam shouted. "I thought we had more time with you."

"At least we're here now!" Claire chimed in.

"And the Historian didn't exactly say you can't come and visit *us*," Liv said.

The rest of the ride back was pretty quiet. Everyone rode on their unicorn or dragon, and even though there wasn't a whole lot more to be said, they held on a little tighter than normal as they rode back to the Unicorn Kingdom.

It went by way too fast for everyone's liking. Before they knew it, they were all walking down to the cell that held Star.

When they arrived, they were so happy that she no longer had fangs or glowing, purple eyes.

"Anyone know why I'm locked up in this dungeon?" Star asked as everyone walked down.

"It's a really long story, but we are so glad to have you back," Moonbeam answered.

They got Star out of the dungeon, and six humans and one dog greeted her with loving embraces.

"You did it, Ava. You saved everyone," Liv said with a smile on her face.

"No, we did it together," Ava answered.

Liv started to feel her eyes fill with tears again. "It's time for us to go home," she said.

Ava threw her arms around Brooke's neck and said, "Don't forget about me, okay?"

"I couldn't forget you if I wanted to," Brooke said.

Neon lowered himself to the ground so Mason could get off. "Bye-bye, horsey," Mason said as he patted Neon on the head.

"Listen to me, Drew," Claire said. "You're going to have a hard time remembering things for a while. But if you ever feel lonely or scared, just try to remember me and this conversation. It is going to get better, but it's just going to take time."

Drew tilted his head to the side like a confused puppy. "I have no idea what you're talking about, but I'll try my best to remember."

"Maybe you'll be able to fly a little faster and farther without me on your back," Grace told Sparkles as she hugged her goodbye.

"I doubt it," Sparkles responded.

Reagan hopped off George the Dragon's back and patted him on the head. "Now you remember what I taught you. We don't burn things. We don't eat unicorns. We eat veggies."

George nodded and then scooped Reagan up to give her a giant dragon hug.

"You've got to come and visit every now and then, okay?" Liv said as she wrapped her arms tightly around Moonbeam. "You're going to be a great queen."

Moonbeam nodded. "Thank you, Liv. I will never forget how brave you, your family, and your friends were."

Liv looked down and saw Leo. She realized that this was the last time she'd be able to talk to him. When they got home, he'd only be able to bark again, and she felt sad about that. Being able to talk to her dog was one of her favorite parts about being in the Unicorn Kingdom.

Leo could sense that something was wrong with Liv, as dogs often do.

"Hey, what's the matter?" Leo asked as he plopped down at Liv's feet.

"I am just sad that I won't be able to talk to you anymore once we get home. I love talking to you, Leo," Liv said.

"Oh, come on. It's no big deal. You went forever without talking to me before."

"Good point," Liv admitted.

"Tell you what. If I'm mad, I'll growl. If I'm worried, I'll bark. And if I'm happy, I'll do this," Leo said as he wagged his tail furiously.

Liv patted Leo on the head. "That sounds just perfect, Leo."

"I'll be the one to take them back," Neon said. "Everyone grab on."

Liv, Ava, Claire, Mason, Reagan, and Grace all put a hand on Neon. Leo walked in front and leaned into Neon's front leg.

Neon's horn started to glow brightly. Within a moment, it was so blinding that Liv had to shut her eyes. The familiar feeling of being lifted and then dropped on her feet happened, and when she opened her eyes, she was standing in her backyard in Andover.

"Listen, kids," Neon started. "I can't thank you enough. If it wasn't for you, I'd probably still be locked up in that dungeon, and now I'm the king of the Unicorn Kingdom. King! Can you believe it?"

"You deserve it," Liv said.

Neon scraped his front hoof in the snow like he was stalling. "What I'm trying to say is that I will take great care of the Unicorn Kingdom and everyone in it until we can fix King Andrew."

"We know you will," Ava replied.

"King Neon!" Mason yelled.

"We'll come back when we can. We'll see you around," Neon said. His horn glowed brightly, and Liv had to shut her eyes again. When she opened them back up, Neon was gone.

CHAPTER 13

DESTINY

A few days had gone by, and Liv was kind of surprised that she hadn't heard from any unicorns. Nobody had come to visit—not one unicorn. She thought a lot about how glad she was that they were able to save their friends and their secret world, especially considering she and everyone except Ava, King Andrew, and Neon were turned into vampires at one point.

Liv also thought about how odd it was that they were able to save an entire world, and then they barely got to say goodbye and were banished forever. Liv knew she was being impatient. So much was going on back in the Unicorn Kingdom.

The unicorns were still probably trying to take care of Drew now that his horn was broken again and he could barely remember his own name. There was still so much work to do. How much of the world was destroyed during the battle and needed to be rebuilt? What were they going to do with the Sword of Ridder? Liv remembered that Ava had placed it on the ground right before they left, and nobody else could move it. What were they going to do with the orbs? Were Moonbeam and Neon doing a good job ruling as king and queen?

Liv knew she was being kind of selfish and maybe even a bit of a baby about not hearing from the unicorns. Deep down, she was certain they would come and visit on Earth just as soon as they could.

Despite all this, the thing that Liv was struggling with the most was knowing she wouldn't be able to talk to Leo again. Every morning he ran up to the girls and wagged his tail furiously like he always did. He almost appeared to be smiling. He made some cute little yelping noises and tried to sneak in some kisses when the girls let their guards down. Liv knew he was trying to tell them something, and she wished he could talk.

"I miss being able to talk to Leo," Liv said quietly one morning when just she and her sisters were awake.

"Me too," Claire replied as she scratched Leo under his chin.

"You know, we are pretty lucky," Ava pointed out. "I bet we're the only people who have ever gotten to talk to their dog."

Even though Liv was still a little sad, that did make her feel better. "Good point, Ava."

Days continued to go by with no visit from the unicorns. It got to the point that Liv started to worry that something might actually be wrong.

Days turned into weeks, and weeks turned into months.

Liv thought about how she felt kind of like a kid again. It was like when she was little and got so excited about her birthday when it was a month or two away. But when you're little, a month or two feels like forever. The worst part about this was that they didn't know when they would see the unicorns. It started to feel like each day was a disappointment.

Every day at school, the girls touched base at lunch. They tried to talk quietly so nobody would hear what they were saying.

Liv lowered her voice to a whisper. "We didn't see or hear anything again last night. How about you guys?"

Reagan shook her head no. "Nothing at my house," she said.

Everyone turned to Grace, who had a disappointed look on her face. "Same with me. Sorry, guys."

A few more days went by without a glimpse of a unicorn.

One night, just when Liv was about to give up and thought she'd never see Moonbeam or another unicorn ever again, she heard a tapping on her window.

For a moment, her heart picked up speed. *Was that a unicorn?* she thought to herself. She glanced out her window, but it was dark and hard to see. She decided it was probably just the wind or something else, and then she heard the tapping again. It was a little louder this time.

She stood up and hurried over to her window. She saw Brooke standing outside in her backyard, smiling at Liv through the window.

Liv cracked her window open. "I am *so* glad to see you!" she whispered.

"Oh my gosh! Same here," said Brooke.

"Can I go get my sisters and sneak outside to talk to you for a bit? They'll want to see you too.'

"Of course," Brooke said, "but go fast because I don't have long."

Liv ran upstairs as quickly and quietly as she could and burst through her sisters' door.

"Liv! Have you ever heard of knocking?" Ava asked sarcastically as she stared at her older sister over the top of the book she was reading.

Liv tried to stay calm and quiet so they wouldn't draw their parents' attention. "Don't freak out, but Brooke is outside and wants to talk to us."

Ava slammed her book shut and shouted, "For real?"

"Shh!" Liv and Claire both said at once.

Claire sprang up out of bed. "Come on. Let's go hear what she has to say."

The three sisters snuck back downstairs and out the sliding glass door that led to their backyard where Brooke was waiting.

All three girls ran over to her and wrapped her up in a hug. They were so excited that they all started talking at once.

"What took you so long?"

"How is Drew doing?"

"Are Moonbeam and Neon making a good king and queen?"

Brooke giggled. "I'm excited to see you guys too. So much has happened, and I'm really sorry it's been so long since we were able to visit."

Liv took a breath and waited for her sisters to ask. Nobody said anything, so she did. "What took you so long?"

"We've been very busy with everything going on back home," Brooke replied. "I don't even have time to tell you everything, but I have a few things I *need* to tell you."

Claire interrupted and asked a second time, "How is Drew doing?"

"Not so good. Well, not so good right now, but that's part of the reason I'm here," Brooke said, getting excited.

"Not so good now, meaning he's going to get better?"

"He is. Moonbeam had a baby!"

Liv, Ava, and Claire looked at each other. Then they all looked at Brooke. The three girls and their unicorn friend all started squealing with excitement.

"That is *amazing*!" Liv exclaimed.

Claire smiled. "Once that baby unicorn is old enough, it'll be able to heal Drew's horn."

"I cannot wait to see their baby unicorn," Ava said." Oh my gosh! It'll be so cute."

"Moonbeam and Neon actually sent me here to tell you the news," Brooke shared. "They want you to meet their child."

"When?" all the girls asked at the same time.

"We were thinking you could have a sleepover with Reagan at Grace's place, and then we can meet you at the tree house," Brooke suggested. "Maybe tomorrow night?"

It was Thursday, and Liv was sure they'd be able to meet at Grace's for a Friday night sleepover.

"We'll be there," Liv replied.

"What did you guys do with the orbs?" Ava asked Brooke.

"After you left, it was like the Sword of Ridder wasn't as magical anymore," Brooke answered. "Goltry was able to lift it, and he brought it back to the statue of Ridder in the Elven Kingdom. Now that we know how important the orbs can be, each was returned to its original kingdom for safekeeping."

"Any more signs of vampires?" Liv asked.

"Not a one!" Brooke said happily. "The Historian thinks that as long as we keep humans out of our world, that kind of evil won't be able to find its way back in. He is still convinced that having humans in our world somehow opened up a gate or portal or something that let bad stuff in.

The girls knew they couldn't go back to the Unicorn Kingdom, and being reminded about it didn't make them feel any better.

Seeing the disappointment on their faces, Brooke quickly changed the subject. "Guess what else?" the unicorn asked.

"What?"

"Moonbeam and Neon made up a holiday in honor of you guys saving the world."

The girls' jaws dropped. "No way! That is so awesome," Ava replied.

"It's called Courage Day in honor of all of you for being so brave and saving us," Brooke said excitedly. "Everyone is going to gather at the Unicorn Kingdom for a giant celebration every year on the anniversary of the day you saved us so we never forget what you did."

Claire was beaming, "That is the craziest thing ever."

Liv giggled. "That's the craziest thing ever so far."

"I've got to get going," Brooke said suddenly. "Make sure you guys are at the tree house tomorrow night so you can meet the baby princess."

Brooke's horn started glowing so brightly that the girls had to close their eyes. When they opened them, Brooke was gone.

Everyone was too excited to sleep, so they called Reagan and Grace and got their sleepover plans lined up.

The next day at lunch, they all sat down together like always. They were grinning from ear to ear.

"Did you convince your parents to let us crash in the tree house tonight?" Liv asked Grace excitedly.

"Sure did. We're golden!"

As soon as school was over, everyone packed their things to get ready for their sleepover. The girls ate dinner, and the second their mom and dad let them leave, they hopped on their bikes and rode to Grace's house.

Liv, Ava, Claire, Grace, and Reagan all hung out in the tree house chatting, laughing, and eating snacks, trying to pass the time until the sun went down. They had a wonderful evening, and before they knew it, it was dark.

Liv heard a whisper from below. "Psst! Are you guys up there?"

All five girls popped their heads over the edge of the tree house floor and saw Brooke at the base of the tree.

"Come down here. Follow me," she told them.

The girls climbed down. Ava jumped onto Brooke's back, wrapping her arms around her unicorn's neck for a giant hug. Brooke led everyone a little farther away from Grace's house toward the woods. On the edge of the woods, Moonbeam, Neon, and Sparkles were waiting.

Liv couldn't see a baby unicorn anywhere.

"We're so excited to see you," Neon said with a giant smile on his face.

Moonbeam smiled at Liv and then looked at Claire. "She is the first unicorn born since Drew's horn was broken. When she gets older and learns her once-in-a-lifetime ability to heal, she'll be the one to save him."

"Since she's destined to heal Drew and make him king again, we named her Destiny," Neon said.

He and Moonbeam were standing side by side. They each took a step back, revealing the cutest unicorn the girls had ever seen.

Destiny was about a quarter the size of a full-grown unicorn. The top of her horn barely reached the base of Neon's chest. The fur on her body was black like Neon's. She resembled Moonbeam as well because her mane and tail were light blue. Her horn was multi-colored like Moonbeam's.

Destiny walked toward the girls so they could see her better in the light of the Minnesota moon. On her dark black fur there was the image of a blue snowflake on her front right shoulder. It looked like a tattoo that many other unicorns had.

The girls could not believe how beautiful Destiny's eyes were. They seemed too big for her head, like she still had to grow into them. But even though they looked big, they didn't look weird. They looked adorable. Her eyes sparkled like the stars above.

"I know who you are," Destiny said in a somewhat high-pitched, childish voice. "You're the reason we celebrate Courage Day. My mom and dad told me all about you."

The girls were in awe of Destiny's cuteness.

"Which one of you is Claire?" Destiny asked.

Claire raised her hand.

"Drew wanted me to tell you that he misses you."

Claire giggled, happy to hear that Drew still remembered who she was.

"Tell him I miss him, too, and I can't wait for him to get better again."

Destiny stepped forward. "I'm not old enough yet, but once I am, I will heal him. I promise," she told Claire.

"Thank you," Claire said, smiling.

Liv was always the one thinking ahead and asking questions, and tonight was no different. "Any idea how long it might take for her to be ready?"

"It's a little different for every unicorn, but most learn their power to heal by the time they're 20 years old," Moonbeam said.

"Twenty years?" Claire said in shock. "That'll take forever!"

"No, Claire, that's 20 years in unicorn time," Liv replied. "Since every hour on Earth is one day in the Unicorn Kingdom, Destiny will be turning 20 in about . . ." Liv had to think for a moment. ". . . about 300 days in Earth time."

"Sweet!" Ava said. "That's not even a year here. That isn't so bad, Claire."

Neon spoke up again. "We're so glad that Destiny will be able to help Drew, and we're thrilled you all got to meet her. We also wanted to come here to thank you once more."

"Things are getting better every day. If it weren't for all of you, your brother, and Leo, life as we know it would have ended," Moonbeam said.

"We are so grateful for everything you've done for us," Neon continued. "We have to head home now, but we'll be in touch when Destiny is ready. Once she's able to heal Drew, we'll bring everyone back to the tree house and heal him in Grace's backyard."

Liv gave Moonbeam a hug goodbye. Grace squeezed Sparkles. Ava gave Brooke another snuggle and then jumped off her back. Since George didn't come with them, Reagan hugged Neon.

"Tell George I miss him, okay?" Reagan asked Neon.

"Of course," Neon said with a smile.

Claire walked up and hugged Destiny. "Don't grow up too fast, little one," she said. "But just as soon as you feel ready, I can't wait for you to heal, Drew."

CHaPTer 14

THE TRUE KING

About a year later, the girls were wondering how much longer it might be until Destiny could heal Drew. They saw the unicorns less often than they had hoped. Usually, a unicorn would swing by at night every few months to give them an update.

"Destiny isn't ready yet, but we think she's really close," a unicorn might say.

"Not yet," said another.

"Maybe soon," added yet another.

These were the types of responses the girls had heard over the last year. They tried to be patient, but it was hard. Claire hadn't seen Drew since the final battle with Luca. All the unicorns worried that with his memory being so bad, he might get scared if he was brought to Earth. They were saving that experiment for when it was time to fix his horn.

The girls wished they could see unicorns once a week like they used to instead of every few months. They all agreed that some visits once in a while were better than never. Even when they brought news that Destiny wasn't ready to heal yet, it was still always such a treat to see Moonbeam, Sparkles, Brooke, and even Star come for a visit.

Over the years, Liv had learned to see the glass as half full instead of half empty. She was looking on the bright side. A little over a year had gone by, and it was now the later part of June in Minnesota. Aside from the beautiful summer weather, it was much easier to coordinate a sleepover during the summer. They could usually convince their parents to let them have a sleepover on a weeknight because school was out.

One summer night when Liv was getting ready for bed, she heard a tap on her window. Many times over the last year, she had thought she heard a tap, but it turned out to be nothing. Her heart always seemed to leap out of her chest as she ran over to her window to see if a unicorn had come to visit.

When she got to the window, she saw Moonbeam standing outside. She opened her window and whispered, "I'll be right out."

"Not tonight. I need to be quick. Destiny is old enough. She thinks she's ready to heal Drew."

"Oh my gosh! That's so exciting! Are we doing it tonight?"

"Not tonight. We're going to do it tomorrow. We'll meet you at Grace's tree house. Can you make sure everyone is there?"

Liv was a little bummed that Moonbeam had to go so quickly, but she was mainly overwhelmed with joy that tomorrow was the big day. "I'll make sure everyone is there," she told Moonbeam. "See you tomorrow."

Moonbeam's horn started to glow, and within moments, she was gone.

Liv snuck upstairs and was about to barge into Ava and Claire's room when she remembered to knock.

"Come in," she heard Ava say.

Liv rushed into the room.

"You knocked! You're growing up, Liv," Claire joked.

"Moonbeam was just here. Tomorrow is the day," Liv practically squealed.

Ava and Claire looked at each other in disbelief, and then they joined in on the squealing.

Liv sent a text message in code to Reagan and Grace. It was the code they agreed to use when this happened.

We have a code pink. Sleepover tomorrow night at Grace's tree house, the text message said.

Everyone had trouble sleeping that night, and for good reason. Liv did find it easier to fall asleep in anticipation of Destiny healing Drew than she did worrying about a battle with a fire-breathing dragon or vampire king. It took a while, but eventually, she was able to doze off.

In the morning, Liv rushed upstairs and found that Ava and Claire were already awake and in the kitchen with Leo. The kitchen was a mess. It looked like they were baking something.

"What are you guys doing?" Liv asked tiredly.

Ava poured some flour into a bowl while Claire stirred. "Remember when we were talking about having a wedding for Neon and Moonbeam, and Drew got super excited about trying cake?" Ava asked.

"Excited about Cheetos cake, to be exact," Claire stated.

Liv laughed. "You guys are making a Cheetos cake?"

"Well, we're trying to," Claire said.

Shortly after that conversation, their mom walked into the kitchen to make some coffee like she normally did in the morning. Seeing the giant mess so early made her raise her eyebrows. "Whatcha doing?" she asked.

"Making a cake," Ava said.

Just then, Claire tore open a bag of crunchy Cheetos. She dumped about half of it into their bowl and started to stir it into the cake batter.

Their mother made a concerned face that only a mom can make. "I think you might be doing it wrong," she said as politely as she could. Claire dropped one more handful of Cheetos into the cake batter and stirred.

"It's kind of an experiment," Ava said.

Ava was always doing experiments of some kind, so their mom wasn't totally surprised by this. She shrugged her shoulders. "Good luck!" she said. "And make sure to clean this mess up when you're done."

The girls baked their Cheetos cake. It was a confetti cake mix with lots of Cheetos added to the batter. They were pleased with how well it baked. They cleaned up their mess while the cake cooled. Once it was cooled down enough, Liv used a butter knife to spread vanilla frosting over the top of the cake.

"It looks like a normal cake after we put the frosting on," Liv said. "You can't even tell there are Cheetos in this thing."

Ava had her elbow on the counter with her chin resting on her hand as she tapped her lip with her pointer finger. "Something is missing," she said.

Claire reached down into the bag of Cheetos and grabbed the small amount that was left. She sprinkled it over the top of the vanilla frosting.

Liv giggled. "This is going to be gross."

"It's perfect," Ava whispered.

After dinner, instead of taking their bikes to Grace's house, they asked their mom for a ride so they could transport the Cheetos cake safely.

"Don't you think you should taste test that thing before you feed it to your friends?" their mom asked.

"No, it's going to be fine," Claire said.

Their mom looked like she wanted to say something. She opened her mouth but then paused for a second and said, "Okay, let's go."

She drove them over to Grace's house. Reagan was already there waiting with Grace. Once their mom left, they carefully brought all their overnight stuff and the cake up to the tree house to wait for the unicorns to arrive.

Time was going by slowly at first, but then Reagan started being hilarious like always. The girls began having a ton of fun. Liv felt like the clock wasn't ticking slower than normal for the first time since she had spoken to Moonbeam the night before.

Soon the sun was setting. It was a beautiful Minnesota summer night in June and the air outside was the perfect temperature. The sky was a combination of pink and purple as the sun set. The clouds seemed to be a shade of pinkish-orange. The girls agreed it was fitting—a perfect evening for an exciting night.

Time continued to fly by, and before long, they started to hear the sound of crickets and frogs that so often had put them to sleep in this tree house over the last couple of years. As the sun dropped below the horizon, the night sky lit up with stars and a full moon.

The girls kept a close eye on the back of Grace's house. They were starting to see the lights turn off in rooms in her home as her parents got themselves ready for bed. Almost the exact moment the last light turned off, they heard a scraping noise at the base of the tree.

The five girls poked their heads over the edge to see Brooke scraping her horn on the tree trunk.

"It's time," Brooke whispered.

"Just a sec," Claire told her. She started to cut the Cheetos cake.

Liv had never heard a cake crunch when it was being cut. She wondered if they put in too many Cheetos.

Before long, Claire had cut their experimental cake into several pieces. They started to slowly and carefully climb down the ladder of the tree house.

Once the five girls and the cake safely reached the bottom, Brooke led them away from Grace's house toward the woods in her backyard.

As they approached the woods, Liv noticed several unicorns. In addition to Brooke were Drew, Moonbeam, Neon, Sparkles, and Destiny.

Destiny looked much older but still fairly young compared to the others. She was about three quarters the size of her mother, Moonbeam.

When Brooke and everyone else stopped, Claire kept on walking up to Drew. "Hey, buddy. We made you a cake," Claire said, not sure whether or not Drew would remember her. Claire picked up two pieces of the cake she had made with her own hands and held one out to Drew.

"Aw, Claire. You shouldn't have," he said.

Claire beamed knowing that Drew still remembered who she was after all this time even though his horn was still broken.

Claire took a bite of her cake. Drew grabbed the other piece and sucked the entire thing down all at once.

The cake crunched as Claire bit into it. Drew crunched loudly on the piece he ate in one mouthful.

Claire winced. "Oh my, this is disgusting!"

"Oh my, this is amazing!" Drew said with his mouth still full, crunching away on his Cheetos cake. He swallowed. "You gonna eat that?" he asked Claire.

"I am not. All yours, buddy," she replied.

Drew crunched through her piece of Cheetos cake. "Wow! You should make these for a living. That was the most delicious thing I've ever eaten."

Claire chuckled. "I'm glad you liked it."

Moonbeam walked over to them and smiled. Neon was by her side, gently holding the piece of Drew's horn in his mouth that Luca had broken so long ago.

"Claire, would you hold that in place while Destiny heals him?" Moonbeam asked.

"Of course," Claire said as she grabbed the piece from Neon's mouth.

Destiny walked up to them. "I'm ready," she said.

Drew knelt down by Claire as she held the broken piece of his horn in place.

Destiny started to chant, *"Once in my life, a miracle to make, it's time now for my power to wake. For in my soul, I can feel it's time to use my power to heal."*

Destiny's horn started to glow the most beautiful shade of pink that the girls had gotten used to seeing over the years. It was somehow both soft and vivid as the glow shot out of her horn to the broken piece Claire was holding in place on top of Drew's head.

Within a few seconds, Claire let go of the horn. It stayed in place as the pink beam continued to go from Destiny to Drew. The beam stopped, and the pink glow faded. Drew's horn was healed, and he stood up.

Everyone erupted with joy.

Destiny stomped her foot on the ground twice. "All hail, King Andrew!" she yelled.

STOMP! STOMP!

The girls knew the drill, so they joined in the stomp.

King Andrew stood there a moment wide-eyed as if his memory was coming back to him all at once. He blinked. He shook his head briefly and then looked around.

"I am so proud of each and every one of you," he said. "I know I am way behind, and I probably have a lot to catch up on. I remember what happened with Luca, and I think every one of you are heroes."

"We're glad to have you back, King Andrew," Neon said as he knelt down.

All the other unicorns knelt too.

"Brooke, Sparkles, tell me—how are things at the Unicorn Kingdom?" King Andrew asked.

"Amazing, actually," Sparkles said.

Brooke nodded in agreement. "Maybe better than ever."

"So these two have done a decent job holding things together since my horn broke?" King Andrew asked, obviously referring to Neon and Moonbeam.

CHRONICLES OF THE UNICORN KINGDOM

"They really have," Brooke said happily.

"They make a pretty amazing team," Sparkles replied.

Neon looked at the ground, appearing to be embarrassed, and Moonbeam blushed.

King Andrew smiled. "You know, I was king for a very long time. If the two of you have been able to hold the Unicorn Kingdom together after everything we've been through, then I think you deserve to keep at it."

Everyone was quiet for a moment and exchanged nervous glances.

"King Andrew," Neon started to say.

"Call me Drew," interrupted Drew. "You have earned this. You are the true king, and as long as you have your queen by your side, you two are going to make our kingdom better than I had ever imagined it."

Moonbeam looked at Neon. Neon looked like he wanted to say something, but he was speechless.

"Thank you for healing me, Destiny," Drew said. "Now, can I have more of that Cheetos cake?"

Everyone started laughing.

It was decided. Drew was going to retire and enjoy life. He would allow Neon and Moonbeam to continue to rule the

Unicorn Kingdom together. Drew ate almost an entire Cheetos cake that night. It was the longest time the girls had spent with the unicorns since they defeated Luca.

They spent the entire night laughing and hanging out on the edge of the woods in Grace's backyard. They never wanted it to end, but eventually, Sparkles noticed the sun was starting to come up.

"We had better get going," Neon pointed out.

Ava hugged Brooke. "I am so glad I got to spend this night with you. I missed you so much. Make sure to come back and visit."

"Every chance I get," Brooke answered.

Reagan walked up and gave Destiny a hug. "Thank you so much for healing Drew. You are a hero."

Destiny smiled and leaned into the hug.

When Destiny was close, Reagan whispered in her ear, "I need you to make sure to take care of George the Dragon for me. Tell him I miss him and that I'll never forget him."

"I'll tell him," Destiny said. "And I promise I'll take care of him for you."

Grace scratched Sparkles behind the ear. "Come back soon, okay?"

"You know I will," Sparkles said.

Liv walked up and gave Moonbeam another hug goodbye. "I wish you didn't have to leave, but I am so glad I got to see you tonight. You and Neon are amazing together. Destiny is beautiful and sweet. And you are queen! I am so proud of you."

"I never thought I could've done any of this," Moonbeam said. "I learned so much about love and bravery from you girls. Thank you so much."

Claire gave Drew the last piece of Cheetos cake, which he devoured.

"You really like that stuff, don't you?" she asked as Drew crunched away.

"Like it? I love it!" Drew replied.

"You know, I think you might be the bravest creature I've ever met," Claire told Drew.

"Funny," he said. "I was just about to tell you the same thing."

Claire gave Drew a giant hug goodbye.

The girls stood back and waved goodbye as the unicorns' horns all started glowing brightly. It got so bright that the girls had to shut their eyes. When they opened them, their unicorn friends had vanished and gone back to the Unicorn Kingdom.

It was silent for a moment.

"We just pulled an all-nighter party in my backyard with *unicorns!*" Grace exclaimed.

"That was the best night ever," Claire said.

Liv smiled from ear to ear. "No, that was the best night ever so far."

CHAPTER 15

THE FINAL CHAPTER

"You're certain that's everything?" the Historian asked.

Bram, Neon, Moonbeam, and Drew all sat across the table from the Historian in the dimly lit library where all of history was kept.

Neon and Moonbeam both nodded.

"Ava and I were the only ones who weren't turned into vampires when it all happened," Drew replied. "I didn't remember exactly everything when my horn was broken, but now that it's fixed, I remember it all."

The Historian paused for a few moments. "It just seems hard to believe."

"I couldn't agree more," Drew answered.

Bram leaned forward and spoke up. He asked the Historian, "Why do you think the girls were able to overcome being vampires and defend their sister when none of the rest of us could?"

"I don't have an answer, but I have a theory," the Historian said. "Actually, it's more of a thought than an actual theory."

"I think it's because humans are capable of loving more deeply than we are," Moonbeam said.

Neon chuckled. "Honestly, Moonbeam, you think they could love each other more than I love you or more than we love Destiny?"

"I think that's exactly right," the Historian replied.

Neon shook his head. "I don't know if we'll ever really know how Liv, Claire, Grace, Reagan, Mason, and Leo were able to save their sister Ava even when they were vampires. But what you're saying doesn't seem possible to me."

The Historian looked down at the final chapter of history he was writing, documenting everything that had happened in their world in order to defeat Luca and save them all from becoming vampires.

"True," said the Historian. "But if what you told me is correct, then here is a list of other things that don't seem possible. These humans and their dog not only helped defeat a dragon but trained it to be their pet. They escaped the mouth of a sea monster to get a lost orb from mermaids. They tracked down the pink unicorn orb that had been lost for hundreds of years. They lost them and got them all back. Ava was the only creature in the world who could lift the Sword of Ridder. Of course, being saved by love doesn't sound possible. None of what I've written here sounds possible."

Neon smiled again. "Well, maybe you're right. They did have a lot of help along the way. But what might be the bravest thing of all is that they never *needed* to help us. They chose to."

The Historian quickly flipped through the book he had written about all the adventures the girls, Mason, and Leo had been on. "Are you sure there is nothing else? Just in case we ever find ourselves in a similar predicament, I want to make sure we can use this account of history to help save us."

Bram spoke up first. "The story is complete and accurate."

Drew thought about Claire and how patient she was with him whenever his horn was broken. He thought about how calm she kept him when his memory was poor and how thoughtful she always was to bring him his Cheetos each time she showed up to visit. "Bram is right," Drew said. "The story is perfect. Everything we need to know in the future is there. But are you sure you captured in your writing how kind they all were?"

The Historian flipped to the back of his book and started writing.

Moonbeam thought about Liv and Ava. So many times they were in seemingly impossible situations, but no matter how tough things got, they leaned on each other and never gave up. "And even though they're small," she said, "they have a lot of fight in them. They would never give up on each other."

The Historian nodded and kept writing.

This got Neon thinking about Mason and Leo. He thought about how funny they always were, even when things got serious. He remembered that the two of them charged in to save the day, never worried about themselves, and always tried to look out for everyone else. "And they're so selfless," Neon said. "They always did anything they could to help and never asked for anything in return."

The Historian picked up the pace of his writing to make sure he was getting everything down.

In the short time that Bram had known these humans and their dog, he had always been impressed, especially after he heard the entire story from Drew, Neon, and Moonbeam over the last several days. It was the same story the Historian was writing down.

"I know we kind of already talked about this, but I am also baffled by their ability to love. Those girls love Reagan and Grace like they were family," Bram said.

"And they loved us like we were family," Moonbeam pointed out.

The Historian nodded and kept writing.

Everyone waited patiently so he wouldn't be interrupted. They wanted to make sure all this was written down because they felt it was important.

Finally, the Historian stopped writing. He looked up. "Anything else?"

"That's everything," Drew replied.

"Wonderful. I can finish up from here. Thank you so much for your help with this. Bram, could you please show them to the door?"

"Of course." Bram got up and started walking out of the library. Neon, Moonbeam, and Drew followed.

Once the door closed, the Historian took a very deep breath. He felt relieved to finally have this very important part of history documented. He spent the next few hours reviewing his work to make sure everything was right and that no details were left out.

He finished his review and then closed the book on what was the most important part of history he had ever written. The cover of the book was, of course, bright pink.

A story this fantastic needs a name, the Historian thought to himself.

He pondered for a moment and then pulled out his quill, dipped it in ink, and wrote *Chronicles of the Unicorn Kingdom* on the cover.

He smiled. It was the first time he had smiled in ages. Even though they weren't there, the humans and their dog were still making a difference. He chuckled and started walking up the stairs to place the book on the shelf.

As he walked, he thought about how impressed he was by what the girls had done. *How could some young humans be such heroes?* He didn't have an answer to that.

He arrived at the shelf that would hold the entire story of Liv, Ava, Claire, Mason, Leo, Reagan, and Grace for years to come. As he placed the book on the shelf, he thought to himself, *I'm not sure how they were able to pull it off, but I am certain that those humans and their dog are the bravest creatures that ever walked the surface of our world.*

ACKNOWLEDGEMENTS

I have so much to be grateful for and so many people to thank! Thank you again to my wife, Ali, for supporting me on this unexpected writing adventure. Thank you to the kiddos for listening to all these bedtime stories over the last few years, and for helping me refine them into something families outside of our home enjoy. Thank you to Linda for the countless, beautiful illustrations you've made along the way to turn our family bedtime story into something far beyond anything we ever imagined. Thank you to the many family members that pushed me to pursue publishing even when I doubted myself. Thank you to Barb for that final push to try!

I also need to thank the professional support I've received along the way. To my Republic Services family – your support has been overwhelming. To the team at Clay Bridges Press, I am grateful for your support, guidance, and expertise I've received countless times over the last few years.

Last, I need to say that I am in absolute awe of the local support we've received since starting this project. We are truly grateful for all the love we've received from our schools, libraries, and readers!

ABOUT THE AUTHOR

Kyle Rawleigh was born in the Twin Cities area of Minnesota. He lives there with his wife, three daughters, and one son. He still enjoys his day job working for a garbage company. When he isn't working, he can be found spending time with his family, being outdoors, cooking, and making up fun stories about unicorns to share with his children. Follow Kyle and his family on Facebook, Instagram, and Twitter @cotukstories.

Enjoy the Full Series!
Have you been a part of the Unicorn Kindom from the very beginning?

Enjoy the beginning of the
adventure in Book #1!
Chronicles of the Unicorn Kingdom series

Saving the King!

Saving the King
Book 1: Chronicles of the Unicorn Kingdom

When three young girls who are living a very normal life in Minnesota try to find a way to save their dog, they find themselves in a very not normal situation. After some odd advice from their unicorn-crazed friend, they end up two worlds away following a unicorn who can barely remember his own name. With a lot of humor, courage, and a bit of magic, they set out to save their dog but wind up leading a revolution to save a world they never knew existed.

Continue the journey in Book #2!
Chronicles of the Unicorn Kingdom Series

Rise of Neon!

Rise of Neon
Book 2: Chronicles of the Unicorn Kingdom

Liv, Ava, Claire, and Grace try to have one normal sleepover with a new friend named Reagan, but things go sideways when their sleepover is attacked by goblins. The girls find out that the Unicorn Kingdom is a lot bigger than they knew. They discover that someone is trying to steal all the pieces of Neon's horn, and they are pulled into another epic adventure to find out who is trying to restore power to the most dangerous unicorn in the Kingdom and stop it from happening.

Return to the Unicorn Kindom in Book #3!
Chronicles of the Unicorn Kingdom series

Werewolf Brother!

Werewolf Brother
Book 3: Chronicles of the Unicorn Kingdom

A freak accident lands the girls in the Unicorn Kingdom with their little brother, Mason. Accidentally teleporting their kid brother to a secret world is just the start of their problems. They take their eyes off him for one second, and he turns into a werewolf! On this adventure, the girls make some new friends in unexplored kingdoms and run across some scary new enemies, including an ancient vampire. Will Liv, Ava, and Claire be able to find a way to un-werewolf their little brother and make it back home before their parents notice they're gone?

www.ingramcontent.com/pod-product-compliance
Lightning Source LLC
Chambersburg PA
CBHW051127260626
47170CB00005B/1704